GUILTY

or

NOT

Also by Alice Zogg

Murder at the Cubbyhole
Revamp Camp
Final Stop Albuquerque
The Fall of Optimum House
The Lonesome Autocrat
Tracking Backward
Turn the Joker Around
Reaching Checkmate

GUILTY
or
NOT

ALICE ZOGG

aventine press

Published by Aventine Press
55 East Emerson St.
Chula Vista CA 91911
www.aventinepress.com

ISBN: 978-1-59330-836-0

Library of Congress Control Number: 2013917272
Library of Congress Cataloging-in-Publication Data
Guilty Or Not/Alice Zogg
Printed in the United States of America

To my longtime friend Pat Yankosky

CREDITS

Credit is due to Patricia Yankosky for showing me her stained glass creations and giving me a step-by-step lesson on how these works of art come into being. I learned a lot about the craft, Pat. If not for Valoise Douglas, I would have had to embark on my research cruise to Alaska alone, missing out on all the fun we shared. Thanks, Val, for having been my travel companion and, as always, an excellent editor of the book. Again, my gratitude goes to my daughter Franziska for proofreading the initial manuscript. I am indebted to the members of the Los Angeles chapter of Sisters in Crime and believe that through their programs, support, and workshops, I continue to hone my craft of writing. Most of all, I appreciate my husband, Wilfried, for putting up with my reclusive behavior, book after book.

CAST OF CHARACTERS

R. A. Huber Private investigator; a lady sleuth par excellence

Peter Huber R. A. Huber's husband; a writer

Antoinette LeJeune (Andi) Huber's assistant; a dynamic young woman

Jonathan Lighthart Hires R. A. Huber; a doctor

Rachel Penrose Accused of killing her fiancé; seems stoic

David Wachterman Rachel's lawyer; a first rate defense attorney

Steven Moretti Murder victim; CEO of restaurant chain

Enzo Moretti Steven's father; founder of the first Cucina di Enzo

Keith Moretti Steven's brother; currently employed on a cruise ship

Jasmine Dewitt Key witness for the prosecution; enjoys the role

Bart Trimboli Steven's childhood friend; remembers the past

Rufina Ramos	Steven's housekeeper; a no-nonsense woman
Marco Valente	Board of Directors member; next in line as CEO
Kevin Gasparian	Board of Directors member; CFO
Claudia Chambers	Board of Directors member; CIO
Tina and Shane Brook	Steven and Rachel's friends; a teacher and a banker
Zack Jefferson	Steven's would-be best man; a software developer
Bo	Andi's new boyfriend; a man of Southern charm

CHAPTER 1

Rachel Penrose's trial for the murder of her fiancé, Steven Moretti, was in full swing on this fifth day of the court proceedings at the Pasadena Superior Court. Rachel sat at the defense table next to her legal counselor, oblivious to the drama unfolding around her. She caught bits and pieces of testimony, but most of it remained a blur to her. Her mind had long shut all emotion out, and she thought, let's just get this over with.

Following the jury selection on Friday, August 10, the actual trial began on Monday, August 13, with opening statements from both the district attorney in charge of the prosecution and Rachel's defense attorney, David Wachterman. There ensued testimony of a string of witnesses called by the prosecution, consisting of police officers, medical doctors and toxicology experts. The twelve jurors plus two alternates paid keen attention, although some of the experts' monologues seemed beyond their comprehension. The authorities had found poisonous oleander mixed in with Steven Moretti's loose leaf tea. Oleander is an evergreen perennial bush containing the toxic glycoside oleandrin, and as little as one leaf of the plant may be toxic enough to cause death in human beings.

Now the prosecution called Rufina Ramos, the housekeeper, as witness to be sworn in by the bailiff. She stated her name and position in the Steven Moretti household, and then the DA performed his direct examination.

Clearly uncomfortable in the limelight, dressed in her new suit, Rufina answered his questions about the tea brewing habits of her employer to the best of her knowledge. His query proceeded to what she saw on April 5 from an upstairs window looking down onto the backyard - - or more to the point, what she failed to see. On cross-examination, David Wachterman wanted to know the exact date of the last tea shipment arriving in the mail as well as its country of origin.

As the housekeeper's testimony evolved, Rachel thought, what difference does it make? They found the damned oleander in the tea, regardless of where the tea was shipped from or how long it had been in the house!

The prosecutor called the next witness, and Jasmine Dewitt strutted up to the witness stand. No denying she looked great in her little black dress and four-inch heels. She had pulled up her blond hair into a demure bun, applied a minimum amount of makeup, and wore understated stud earrings for the occasion, but nothing demure showed in her body language. Obviously, the young woman enjoyed the spotlight.

Rachel tuned out and kept her stoic expression during Jasmine's testimony. Why go through that horrible day once more? She had re-lived it in her dreams and most of her waking hours time and time again. Much easier to ignore it all and retreat into a world of her own. Toward the end of Jasmine's statement, Rachel became aware of sudden silence in the courtroom, which made her come out of her reverie and focus on the proceedings playing out before her.

The prosecutor took a couple of steps closer to the witness stand, lowered his voice a notch, and asked, "Tell us, Ms. Dewitt, what was the defendant's reaction when she walked in on you and Steven Moretti in the bedroom?"

Jasmine replied, "First she just stared, and then she lost her cool."

"Do you remember her exact words?"

"Yes, I do. She pointed at Steven and shouted, 'You disgusting bastard, I'll kill you for this!' and ran out the door."

There were excited murmurs among people in the spectator seats, and the judge called for a lunch recess. Rachel thought, why is everyone surprised? The bimbo told the truth.

Tina Brook, the last person called to testify on that fifth day of the trial, made her way over to the witness stand. Tina and her husband Shane were good friends of Steven Moretti and Rachel Penrose. By no means pleased to appear before the court and jury, Tina had no choice in the matter when subpoenaed. She settled into the stand and had a great shock when briefly glancing down at her friend seated at the defense table. Rachel had dwindled to skin and bones, and the sunken-in eyes told of sleepless nights. Gone were the healthy, outdoorsy complexion and spunky *joie de vivre* attitude.

Tina had only been in the hot seat for about 20 minutes, but the relentless questioning made it seem like hours. The prosecutor grilled her on events as far back as Rachel and Steven's engagement party, which had been such a joyous event that she failed to see his point. Then he switched to the more recent past, and since she was under oath, she had no alternative but to make some statements damaging to her friend.

The DA said, "I understand that you were the person who informed Rachel Penrose of Steven Moretti's death. Correct?"

"That's right."

"How did that come about?"

"I thought that she might not know; naturally, she moved out of the house after what happened. Wouldn't you?"

The judge said, "Please, Ms. Brook, just answer the questions."

"Yes, your Honor."

The prosecutor prompted, "So you called the defendant. Correct?"

"Yes. I couldn't think of a delicate way to put it and just said, 'I have bad news: Steven is dead.'"

"And what did Rachel Penrose reply to that shocking news?"

Tina mumbled something, almost in a whisper.

The judge intervened again, "Speak up, please!"

Tina stated, "She said, 'I hope he rots in hell.'"

Rachel glanced at the jurors and noticed shocked expressions on some of their faces. She mused, why is it so hard for people to accept the truth?

Next to her, the defense lawyer cringed seeing her nod in agreement to Tina's statement. She must be out of her mind, he thought. I'll take a great risk by putting her on the stand. She may go completely berserk and plead guilty. A good thing I don't have to make the decision whether or not I should let her testify this very moment.

The prosecutor stated, "No more questions." And with a hand gesture toward David Wachterman he said, "Your witness."

"No questions; I do not wish to cross-examine."

The DA stated, "The prosecution rests."

The judge excused the jury while the lawyers argued with him over the merit of the evidence.

David Wachterman said, "Your Honor, there is clearly a lack of evidence here. I ask for a motion of demurrer."

The judge did not accept the motion challenging the legal sufficiency of a case against Rachel. After the jury assembled again, he proclaimed, "Court adjourned until tomorrow morning at ten o'clock."

CHAPTER 2

Although the story that led to the trial started long before, this narrative of it begins on a sunny Tuesday in mid-May when R. A. Huber met her new client. As she pulled into the parking lot on that morning, a man paced back and forth in front of her Pasadena office. He stopped pacing and looked at the trim woman with shoulder-length salt-and-pepper hair who came out of her car and walked toward him with a springy athletic gait. She stepped past him, came to a halt at the door with the sign *R. A. Huber, Private Detective*, and inserted the key into the lock. He thought, that can't be her. Must be the secretary. When Nadine had called the investigator "seasoned," he'd assumed the term referred to experience, not age.

Huber turned to him and asked, "May I help you?"

"I need to speak with R. A. Huber."

"That's me. Come on in."

She switched on the lights and disengaged the burglar alarm – which was installed after her office had been broken into – turned on the air-conditioner, and stashed her briefcase and purse in the bottom drawer of her credenza. Then she motioned him to the client seat and offered coffee or water. He declined both, so she sat down in her own chair behind the desk.

Nine out of ten people who came to Huber's office for the first time commented on her Staunton Rosewood chessboard set up with chessmen at one end of her desk. Not so this young man, who came straight to the point.

He said, "I'm Jonathan Lighthart and want to hire you. A friend of mine has been arrested for a murder she did not commit."

"What do you suggest I do in the matter?"

"Find the real killer, of course."

"That simple, you think! The authorities usually have good reason for an arrest. Tell me the details and I'll decide whether or not I can help you. But first, give me some basic information about yourself."

"What do you need to know?"

"Mr. Lighthart, please inform me of your profession, marital status, relationship to the accused, town of residence; that sort of thing." And with a twinkle in her eye she added, "I won't ask for your social security number."

Not amused, he said, "I'm an MD with an internal medicine practice here in Pasadena, and also live in town. I'm single, and my relationship to Rachel is that of an old friend."

"May I ask how you learned about me?"

"You were highly recommended by Nadine Dugat."

Huber reflected for a second and then said, "The name sounds familiar, but I can't place her for the moment."

"I know Nadine professionally. She was the dietitian at *Optimum House* before its downfall. She told me all about how you solved the murders in that place."

"Oh yes, I remember her now; an extremely efficient young woman."

Then she said, "Okay, Doctor, I'm ready to listen to the trouble your friend Rachel is in."

So he began, "Her full name is Rachel Penrose, and I've known her since we were kids. We lived next door from each other when growing up. Last September, she got engaged to Steven Moretti. As a matter of fact, I went to her engagement party. Moretti was the CEO of Cucina di Enzo and - -"

Huber interrupted, "The restaurant chain?"

He nodded and continued, "They set their wedding date for April 14, but ten days before, Rachel found Steven in bed with another woman and apparently threatened to kill Moretti. Rachel had moved into his house some months before. Of course, after walking in on the cheater on April 4, she moved out again. On April 8, Moretti died of poisoning. The autopsy revealed traces of oleander leaves in his system. It so happens that there is an oleander bush in Moretti's backyard, and Rachel is accused of mixing the oleander leaves in with the loose leaf tea he usually drank."

Huber said, "Let me make sure that I've got the time frame correct. When exactly did Rachel move out of Mr. Moretti's house?"

"Right away. She didn't spend another night under his roof."

"As I see it, before April 4, she had no cause to mix her fiancé's tea with oleander, and afterwards, she stayed no longer at his house. So how could she have managed to add the toxic substance to the tea which killed him on April 8?"

"The idea is that she added the oleander to the tea leaves the next day when she went back to pack her stuff."

"I see." Then she inquired, "Was Moretti alone when he died?"

"I believe so, but I'm ignorant of the details."

"Please go on."

"That's all I know. They arrested her a few days later and her trial is scheduled for August."

"Is she in jail?"

"No. Her folks borrowed the money for her bail."

"Will she have a public defender?"

"Her dad can ill afford it, but he hired a first-rate defense attorney. I've talked with him; his name is David Wachterman, and he told me that the situation looks grim for Rachel. That's why I'm here to hire you."

Huber studied him for a long time. By no means handsome, he had a pleasantly agreeable face, perfectly suited for a general practice physician. He had delicate hands, which he kept folded in front of him on top of the desk. He seemed to be under stress, which Huber linked to the situation Rachel was in. The doctor looked extremely young, almost boyish. He must be straight out of medical school, she presumed, wondering if she'd have confidence in someone that age, were she his patient.

She asked, "Do you have somebody in mind as the suspect?"

"No, but there has to be someone other than Rachel with a motive to kill the man."

"Has it occurred to you that she might be guilty?"

"Impossible!"

"You don't think she is capable of murder?"

He took some time before he responded, "I guess, under certain circumstances, anybody could be. Rachel has a temper and if she'd attacked and killed him right then and there in a fit of rage, I'd say that's possible." And he eyed her steadily as he continued, "But premeditated murder? No way!"

Huber stated, "You interest me!" And after a slight pause she said, "I take it that you know Rachel well."

"Better than most people," he replied.

"How old is she?"

"She turned 28 in March."

"You mentioned that you grew up together; so are you approximately the same age?"

"I'm three years her senior. As a kid, she always came running to me when in trouble," and an unexpected smile came over his face as he continued, "even as late as high school."

Huber absentmindedly made an opening move with a white pawn on her chessboard and said, "You need to be straight with me. Are you and Rachel more than just friends?"

He did not rush to answer but rather seemed to carefully mull over the question. He finally said, "If you mean, are we or have we ever been lovers, I can honestly say no. And as far as Rachel goes, I am positive that she only considers me her best platonic friend. As for me, when in elementary school, I loved her as a little sister. During her teen years, I secretly admired her but made sure she had no inkling of it. Ever since she became an adult, I never showed my true feelings for fear that I might lose her friendship."

Embarrassed, he looked away, and Huber said, "It took great courage to tell me this. Thank you."

He still did not meet her eyes, staring at the wall behind her.

Huber thought over his plight for a long moment and then suddenly said, "I've decided to take on Rachel's case. I will do my best to get at the truth, but I'm warning you, the truth may not end up being to your liking."

She eyed him keenly when uttering those words, making sure he understood her meaning.

He looked at her straight on now, and there was no doubt about his perception as he said, "The true facts are all I want. I hope that you can unearth them before Rachel's trial begins."

"I'll talk with her attorney first and then I need to see Rachel herself. So please give me their numbers."

The doctor complied, and then they discussed her fee, which he had no problem agreeing with. They shook hands and Huber promised to keep him posted. On his way out and already at the door, he suddenly turned around and walked back to her desk.

He said, "When you talk with Rachel, please don't tell her who hired you. She has a lot of pride and wouldn't accept such a gift from me."

Huber watched him leave and waited until he closed the door. Then she made a counter-move with the black knight in her solitaire chess game and thought, what an unusual young man!

CHAPTER 3

The law offices of Rosenthal, Wachterman, & Vogel was a busy place. Paralegals rushed about trying to meet deadlines while secretaries furiously hammered away on their computers. The receptionist was hard at work arguing with someone on the phone, so Huber sat down in the reception area.

She looked at the décor. It had obviously been chosen to create an image. The antique coffee table next to her seemed made of solid oak. On the walls hung two impressionist prints by Camille Pissarro, *Boulevard Montmartre* and *Avenue de l'Opera*. Centered between them, she observed an elegant French commode.

At the front desk, the receptionist ended her call and asked, "May I help you?"

"I'm R. A. Huber and have an appointment at noon with Mr. Wachterman."

The receptionist pushed a button on her phone and announced, "I have Mrs. Huber here."

Moments later, a young woman appeared and greeted Huber with, "I'm Pamela, David Wachterman's secretary," and ushered her into an inner sanctum. Huber followed her down a hallway, where Pamela stopped in front of an open door and stepped aside, saying, "Go on in, please."

In contrast to the reception area, Wachterman's office looked plain. The spacious room lacked any kind of ornamentation. There were bookshelves sagging under the weight of legal tomes, a file cabinet, and a large desk cluttered with paperwork and stacks of files. The lawyer, a lanky man in his forties with deep-set gray eyes and brown buzz-cut hair, sat behind his littered desk, pen in hand, writing away, old-fashioned style. He looked up when Huber entered and got to his feet, revealing a bone-colored shirt, a brown-and-blue striped tie, and a tan Armani suit, the jacket of which hung over the back of his chair.

The secretary said, "If you don't need me any longer, I'll take my break."

"Sure, Pam, go ahead," he said, and she left, closing the door.

The lawyer motioned Huber into a chair while settling back into his own.

Huber said, "Thank you for seeing me on such short notice. I'm aware that my appointment is cutting into your lunch time."

He brushed it off with a flip of the hand and then said, "I know what you're all about. I looked you up."

"Oh?"

"Jonathan Lighthart mentioned that he planned to hire a private eye. When you called my secretary for an appointment and mentioned my client, Rachel Penrose, you made me curious. I learned that you are a licensed P.I. with an excellent track record." He looked her in the eye and continued, "I'm still curious; what made someone like you go into that line of business?"

Huber said, "You mean, is this little old lady from Pasadena up to bumping heads with criminals?"

"Something like that," he replied, amused.

"My age and size are actually an advantage. People tend to underestimate me. As it happens, I'm good at detective work. Folks tend to open up to me and part with information they'd hold back when questioned by the authorities. I have an un-muddled mind and can solve puzzles with logic. And most important, I'm stronger than I look and an excellent shot."

He cleared his throat and said, "If you can find us another plausible suspect, more power to you."

"You don't think that's possible?"

"Anything's possible, and we're only in the early stages of discovery, but it looks bleak for Rachel. Although I will argue that the evidence against her is circumstantial, there is no denying that the prosecution has a strong case."

"Do you believe that she is guilty?"

"It doesn't matter what I believe; I'll defend her to the best of my ability."

Huber gave him an intense stare, but he kept a poker face.

She said, "I learned only the main facts from Dr. Lighthart; there is plenty more I need to know before I can start my investigation."

"Go ahead."

"I forgot to ask what Rachel does for a living."

"She is a speech therapist."

"Do you know the name and profession of the other woman?"

"What other woman?"

"I mean the person who had an affair with Steven Moretti."

He fingered among his messy pile of papers in front of him, grabbed a folder and looked inside. Then he gave a brief smirk and said, "An affair is an overstatement. Her name is Jasmine Dewitt and she works at Club Marzipan as a stripper."

"Interesting."

"She'll be the prosecution's key witness."

Huber asked, "May I trouble you about giving me names of the victim's close family, business associates, as well as friends that could have an impact on Rachel's case?"

He laughed now outright and said, "You want it all, don't you!" Then he got serious and continued, "Since we are on the same team, I'll give you the info under one condition: You report back to me as soon as you have a lead."

"Agreed."

"I'll have my secretary send you a list of potential witnesses."

She reached into her purse and, handing him her business card, said, "I appreciate it, thank you."

"Anything else?"

"Who discovered Steven Moretti's body?"

He gave her a puzzled look and then replied, "I guess the paramedics. They tried to revive him, but were too late."

"I take it that he was alone when he died. Did somebody report him missing?"

Wachterman replied, "He called 911 himself."

And peeking at the file in front of him he added, "This is what we know. Moretti called 911 on Sunday, April 8, at 6:30 in the evening, telling the dispatcher that he felt extremely ill. He complained of nausea and vomiting, abdominal pain, and diarrhea, which had started hours earlier. He first thought that he suffered from the 24-hour flu, but then got progressively worse. His heart had been racing, and when he made the call, he felt drowsy. By the time the paramedics got to him, he had apparently had a seizure, ending in a coma that led to his death."

Huber said, "That report definitely puts me in the picture. I presume that the authorities found oleander leaves mixed in with Steven Moretti's loose leaf tea he drank that day. Correct?"

"That is so. The poisonous leaves had been cut down to the same size as the tealeaves and were found blended in with the tea in the canister where Steven Moretti kept it. The police also discovered the used substance in the victim's trash. And of course, the autopsy revealed oleander in his stomach."

She asked, "Had Mr. Moretti made a will?"

"None came to light as far as we know. I will point out to the jury that the two had not been married yet, so Rachel Penrose is not inheriting Moretti's money. And I'm sure the prosecution will claim that this was not a murder for gain, but rather a passion crime."

He looked at his watch and asked, "Anything else?"

"No, I think that's it. I'll see Rachel Penrose to start with, and then I'll go from there."

"Good luck. I hope you'll get through to her."

"Why do you say that? Is she uncooperative?"

"Unapproachable is more like it."

"How do you mean?"

"You'll see for yourself."

CHAPTER 4

Peter and Regula Huber's longtime home stood in a town called Merida, located in the San Fernando Valley at the foot of the Angeles National Forest Mountains. Merida, in spite of its population of barely 10,000, boasted a variety of excellent restaurants, their favorite being *Chez Tante Jeanne*. On Wednesday evening, the couple opted to have dinner there.

Maurice - - owner, host, and maître d' all in one - - came to greet them at the door and escorted them to their table, saying, "So nice to see you both!"

R. A. Huber decided on trout amandine and her spouse chose osso buco. They savored their respective meals and only after they had finished and ordered coffee did they start to converse.

Peter said, "So what's the occasion for dining at a fancy place in the middle of the week during a recession?"

She smiled and replied, "I had two reasons for suggesting it. Number one, I wanted to cheer you up."

"Who said I need cheering up?"

"Come now, Peter, you've been down in the dumps for days. Forget the not-so-favorable review of your latest book; after all, it's the opinion of just one person."

"*Not-so-favorable?* It was a horrendous review! My integrity as a writer came under attack."

"Okay, so the reviewer made some disparaging remarks, but like I said, it's only his opinion. Your book is a good read and you'll soon get positive feedback from your fans."

"I hope you're right. Thanks for the pep talk; I needed it. And to show you what a good sport I am, I've decided to take the reviewer's criticism to heart and learn from it."

"That's the spirit!"

Seated across from him, she glanced at his familiar features with appreciation. He had long turned prematurely gray, but now his hair gleamed snow white, and even his prominent eyebrows and mustache were getting lighter. The only thing unchanged over the years was his hazel eyes, forever steady and holding strength of character.

The waitress brought their coffees and then Peter asked, "So what's the other reason we're here?"

"Oh, I didn't get a chance to go grocery shopping and fix us dinner."

He gave off a hearty laugh, which made her realize that his moping mood had passed, and his good-humored self was fully restored.

Then he said, "Enough talk about me, how was your day?"

"It started by my getting beaten at racquet ball."

"I guess you can't always win," he teased, "after all, you're getting older."

"Getting older is no excuse; I wasn't much younger last week when I won."

"Good point! So how did your interview with the lawyer go?"

"It went surprisingly well. Stuck in traffic on the 405 driving to the West Side, I had plenty of time to think. I started to have doubts that Mr. Wachterman would give me any useful information."

Peter interjected, "I didn't know that you had to drive that far. Where on the West Side is his office?"

"It's right on Wilshire Boulevard, close to UCLA."

"You could have paid Andi a visit."

"I thought about it on my way home, but decided not to call her since she'd probably be in class."

She picked up her train of thought again and continued, "Anyhow, when I called the attorney's office yesterday, I only spoke with his secretary, and, on the drive over I suddenly feared that he may be tight-lipped and brush me off with declarations of lawyer/client confidentiality. I looked them up beforehand and learned that Rosenthal, Wachterman, & Vogel is a well-established law firm, and that its partners and associates all have excellent reputations. To my pleasant surprise, it turned out that Mr. Wachterman and I had a satisfying talk."

Peter put in, "Don't forget, he and his client benefit if you come up with another viable suspect."

"Yes, I'm sure he realizes that. He said that we were on the same team. However, I got the distinct feeling that he does not think I'll find another murderer. In his opinion, there is too much evidence against Rachel."

"Does he believe that his client is guilty?"

"He didn't admit as much but I came to that conclusion."

"You've got a tough job ahead, Regula!"

"That's me; always up for a challenge."

CHAPTER 5

When R. A. Huber got to her office on the next day, she determined to learn a bit more about Rachel Penrose before setting up an interview with her. She called Jonathan Lighthart, and the receptionist told her that he was in consultation with a patient, but would she like to talk to the nurse. Huber insisted that she needed to speak with the doctor himself and left her name and number. Meanwhile, she got busy with some office chores, mainly preparing a bill for the client of her last case.

Then she checked her e-mail and saw a message from Pamela of Rosenthal, Wachterman, & Vogel, which read, "Attached is a list of potential witnesses we have so far in the Rachel Penrose file. I left out the police officer who made the arrest since there is no chance that he would give you information before Rachel's trial. I also did not include the expert witnesses, who Mr. Wachterman feels you are not interested in. Good luck, Pamela."

Huber opened the attachment and to her delight found a list of names, complete with numbers, e-mail addresses, snail-mail addresses, and each person's relationship to the late Steven Moretti. She quickly pressed the reply key on her computer and wrote, "Thank you so much. R. A. Huber."

Once more, she went over the information carefully. Listed as relatives and persons of interest of the murder victim were his father, who lived in San Diego; his brother, with an e-mail address but no phone number or place of residence noted next to his name; several board of directors of the Cucina di Enzo Corporation; friends of Steven and Rachel; a housekeeper; and of course, Jasmine Dewitt.

She smiled to herself when she thought of the wording in the e-mail. She could picture the lawyer telling his secretary, "Don't include the expert witnesses, they're none of her business." In fact, Huber felt more than happy with the information at hand. Interviewing expert witnesses would have cost her a steep sum, if they'd have agreed to talk to her at all. And the benefit of such interviews would be doubtful.

She was about to take the first bite from her sack lunch when Jonathan Lighthart returned her call. Before she got a chance to say anything, he asked, "Have you already made a discovery that will help Rachel?"

"I don't work that fast. What I need is some more input from you about Rachel."

"Sure."

He only uttered that one word, but Huber could hear the disappointment in his voice. She said, "You gave me Rachel's phone number, but no address. Where did she move to when leaving Steven Moretti?"

He replied, "She temporarily stays with her parents, who live in Monrovia. The number I gave you is her cell phone."

"Something else. Did you see her after her arrest?"

"Only once, and she is a changed person."

"I can imagine that the drama of being charged with murder would change most people's attitude."

"Of course, but it's more than that. She used to be full of energy and animation, and now all her pep is gone. She seems to have given up without a fight; that's just not like her. It's almost as - -" he stopped himself.

Huber finished the sentence for him "- - as if she were guilty?"

"No, no!" he shouted into the phone, "I don't accept that."

Then he said in a normal tone of voice, "Is there anything else you need from me? I have a patient waiting."

Huber replied, "Just one more question. You told me that you went to Rachel's engagement party, so you knew Steven Moretti. What did you think of him?"

He paused for a long time before he answered, "I only met him twice, so I can hardly say that I knew him. He was friendly enough on both occasions, but I didn't like him. I got the impression of an aggressive man, always taking what he wanted."

On that note they ended the call.

CHAPTER 6

When scheduling an interview with Rachel Penrose, Huber left it up to the young woman where she would rather have the talk: in Monrovia at her folk's house, at R. A. Huber's office, or meet at a Starbucks somewhere in between. Rachel chose the detective's office in order to have privacy. They set the date for the coming Monday, one of Rachel's short days at work, and she would swing by on her way home.

She promptly arrived at the appointed time of 3:15 in the afternoon. There was grace in her movements as she walked to the client chair and sat down. She had a slender athletic figure, high cheekbones, and light-blue eyes that made a striking contrast to her dark hair. Those eyes held a haunted look of late.

To put her at ease, Huber said, "I understand that you are a speech therapist. I am unfamiliar with that profession. What education is needed for the job?"

She replied, "One needs a master's degree in either communication sciences or communication disorders. The next step is to complete between 300 and 400 hours of clinical training, pass a national exam, and finish at least nine months of professional experience after graduation.

In addition, most speech therapists take educational courses. I took mine in child language disorders and stuttering."

"So you work with children?"

"Yes, I provide my services in elementary schools here in Pasadena, helping students improve their language and communication skills. I work with children one-on-one or in groups to treat voice disorders, stuttering problems or learning disabilities."

"I take it that you like your job."

"Yes, I do. It can be rewarding." The haunted look in her eyes intensified as she added, "Working has become difficult for me lately."

"How so?"

"Parents and sometimes even students have been giving me strange looks ever since I got arrested. You can't keep being accused of murder a secret." She suddenly realized why she had come to R. A. Huber's office and said, "Pops shouldn't spend so much money on me; I'm not worth it."

Huber failed to correct her, letting her think that her father had done the hiring.

She asked, "Are you an only child?"

Rachel nodded, then continued with her previous argument, "It's useless; we're wasting your time." And she stared in front of herself.

Huber became aware that Rachel clammed up and raised her voice a tad to get her attention, saying, "I am going to be honest with you. I had a talk with your lawyer, David Wachterman, and he told me that you are unapproachable. Is that true?"

She took some time before she raised her eyes to meet Huber's and said, "He bombards me with questions every time we meet."

"He asks you questions that you either won't or can't answer, and so you keep silent?"

"I guess so."

"Mr. Wachterman is trying to help you. He can't defend you properly if he doesn't know all about you and your circumstances. I am willing to help too, if you let me."

Rachel did not answer, but went on instead, "My life fell to pieces on that horrible day. I've been numb ever since."

"You mean on the day you caught your fiancé and the other woman in the act?"

Rachel re-lived the scene in her mind. She had come home early from her final wedding gown fitting. The gown, like all else planned for the big wedding reception on the Queen Mary, docked in Long Beach, had turned out perfect, and she literally glowed with anticipation for their big event. She had entered the house announcing, "I'm home, hon," slamming the door behind her. When Steven was nowhere to be found on the ground floor, she ran up the stairs, taking two steps at the time. Finding the bedroom door ajar, she'd walked toward it, and pushing it open, proclaimed, "Guess what, I..." she had stopped dead at the threshold and stared in total shock. When her brain functioned again, all she could think was, *I want you dead!*

Huber eyed her keenly, waiting for an answer.

Rachel suddenly shook herself, the way a dog does when coming out of water. Then she said, "Yes, that day."

"I know this is painful for you, but I need to ask you personal questions in order to fully grasp the situation. What town did you and Steven live in?"

"He bought a house in La Cañada Flintridge, and I moved in after we got engaged."

"How long had you known each other and where did you meet?"

"We belonged to the same ski club and met in Mammoth over two years ago." And a sudden spark lit up her blue eyes when she added, "We spent a glorious week challenging one another to all the double black diamond runs on the mountain. At the end of a particularly fun day, chasing me down *Wipeout Chutes* under chairlift 23, he said, 'You are the first woman I'd like to spend my life with.'"

The expression on her face turned stoic again as she stated, "I don't want to talk anymore about Steven; I thought I had erased him from my memory."

Then Huber inquired, "Did you know Jasmine Dewitt beforehand?"

Rachel momentarily drew a blank with the name. Then she said, "Oh, you mean the bimbo? No, I'd never seen her before."

"How about earlier? Were there other indiscretions on Steven's part during your relationship?"

"Steven made no secret of the fact that he had a long, sordid past where women were concerned. Stupid me, I believed that he'd left that all behind..."

Rachel became silent and stared into space with that blank, passive look of hers.

Huber waited, seemingly having all the time in the world.

Rachel looked around the room, focusing briefly on the French Country art prints hanging on the wall she faced, and then fixed her gaze on the chess figures set up at one end of the desk.

She remarked, "You have an exquisite chess set here."

Huber thought, aha. This young woman is not as oblivious as she seems.

Aloud she said, "Thanks, the set holds special memories for me: I inherited it from my father."

The detective in Huber needed to get to the gist of the matter, so she said, "I know that you went back to Steven's house the next day to pack your things. Who let you in?"

"I still had a key and let myself in."

"So you were alone in the house?"

"No, being a Thursday, Rufina, the housekeeper, was there."

"Did you talk to her?"

"Sure, she offered to help me, but I preferred being left alone. So I packed my bags and boxes, made a few trips to the car and back, left my key in the foyer, and was out of the place for good."

"You had no furniture in the house belonging to you?"

"We had selected the furnishings together, but Steven paid for it all. None of it belonged to me. The pile of wedding presents stood unopened in a spare room, and of course the gifts are all being returned. I went to the backyard, though, and dug up my herb garden, taking the plants home to Monrovia."

"Why did you do that?"

"My herb garden was my pride and joy - - still is - - and I had accumulated plenty of exceptional plants and didn't want them to go to waste."

"I see."

Then Huber studied her carefully as she asked, "Did you do anything to the oleander bush in the yard?"

Rachel kept quiet, reassuming her impassive demeanor.

"Do you know where Steven Moretti kept his loose leaf tea?"

"Of course. I lived in the same house. He kept it in an airtight tea canister on the kitchen counter."

"Did he add anything to his tea as a rule?"

Rachel gave her a blank stare.

"What I'd like to know is, did he take sugar, milk, or maybe lemon with his tea?"

"He added honey."

"Did you ever drink any yourself?"

"I prefer coffee."

"What about the oleander in the backyard?" Huber repeated. "Did you go near it on that day?"

Again, Rachel gave no answer and stared straight ahead, ignoring the question.

Huber had a great urge to take the woman by the shoulders and shake her violently. She resisted the temptation and instead raised her voice and snapped her fingers ten inches in front of the other's face, insisting, "Tell me about the oleander plant in the garden!"

At last, Rachel looked Huber in the eye and murmured, "I knew that oleander is poisonous and thought; *what if - -?*"

There followed a long pause while Huber reflected on the meaning of the "what if" aspect.

She finally asked, "Did you make use of that knowledge?"

Rachel did not seem to grasp the significance of that question and once more retreated into her own world, never snapping out of it until Huber concluded the interview.

CHAPTER 7

The Hubers enjoyed a leisurely evening at their home, relaxing in the living room on their respective recliners. Peter immersed himself in one of his colleague's work of fiction, while Regula played games on her Nintendo DS.

She suddenly exclaimed, "I beat my own *Big Brain* top score!"

Peter looked over at her and said, "You're a kid at heart! I'm always amazed at your enthusiasm when playing games."

"Well, this one not only helps me think clearly but also makes my brain react at a fast pace. Both abilities come in handy in detective work."

Peter laughed out loud. "As long as you have a good excuse!"

Then he inserted the bookmark into the current page of his read, closed it, and said, "Tell me about your interview with the accused murderess."

R. A. Huber had learned long ago that she benefited from discussing her cases with Peter. On top of appreciating him as a good listener, she valued his input. Having the talk with Rachel Penrose fresh on her mind, she related all of it to him.

Peter paid keen attention and when her narrative ended, he thought about it for a moment before asking, "Do you think her tuning in and out was all an act?"

"It seemed genuine, but I could be wrong. She reminded me of a child who, although not admitting to any wrong doing, is ready to take the punishment."

"So you believe that she's guilty?"

"Not necessarily. She may feel guilty without having committed the crime. On the other hand, she may well be responsible for the killing."

"You're making no sense, Regula."

"I know; I'm expressing myself badly. The truth is; I haven't sorted things out yet in my own mind."

Peter said, "Considering her education and job, she sounds like an intelligent person. She must be aware of the consequences if a jury finds her guilty. Why then doesn't she assert her innocence? When you asked her about the oleander bush, for instance, why didn't she simply state that she hadn't cut off any leaves to poison Moretti with?"

"Why indeed?" his spouse replied.

Then Peter remarked, "Statistically, poison is a female's choice of weapon."

"Yes, I know. But then, a potential killer might have been aware of that statistic too if he wanted to frame Rachel with that oleander business."

"So you think she may have been set up?"

Regula shrugged and said, "There is so much more information I need to gather before I can form an opinion on that."

Peter remarked, "Come to think of it, the oleander plant is not uncommon. I've seen it on median strips of California highways."

"What does it look like?"

"It's a shrub with attractive white or pinkish-red blossoms."

"I may have seen it without knowing what kind of plant I was looking at."

Then she got back to her main subject and said, "The interview frustrated me in a lot of ways, but I also learned a few interesting things about Rachel and her late fiancé. The pair even has something in common with us."

"Such as?"

"Skiing the black diamonds at Mammoth."

"That's definitely a point in her favor," he said with a chuckle.

As Peter turned back to his book, Regula got up and announced, "I'm going to call Andi. I don't know yet whether I'll need her help with this job, but I'll give her the skinny, just in case. Besides, I haven't seen her in a while and sure miss her." That said, she disappeared from the room and proceeded to call her dynamic young assistant.

She stepped back into the living room three quarters of an hour later. Peter looked up from his read and remarked, "You must have told her the Rachel story, and then some!"

"I sure did, and Andi had exciting news of her own. She has a boyfriend."

"And that's earth-shattering news?" Peter asked amused.

"For her it is. You must know that she's dated plenty of guys since she's been at UCLA, but until now she hadn't called anyone her boyfriend."

"So it's serious?"

"Possibly. I should have guessed something was up when she forgot about target shooting practice last month."

"She didn't show up for her favorite activity! The girl must be on cloud nine. Is the boyfriend in one of her classes?"

"He's not a student. She said he reminds her of her daddy."

"Uh-oh! Where did they meet?"

"At the Harley-Davidson dealership when she took her bike in for servicing."

Peter asked, "The guy's a salesman?"

"No, a customer."

"Well, let's hope he's not a Hell's Angels gang member."

CHAPTER 8

To get a feel for the ambiance, Huber first planned to show up at Club Marzipan unannounced and ask for Jasmine. After some reconsideration, she decided against it. If the young woman had a stage name, she'd be at a loss whom to ask for. Plus, given her gender and age, she would have stuck out like a sore thumb at the club. Jasmine Dewitt lived in Studio City, and when Huber called to schedule an appointment, the entertainer told her to drop by anytime as long as it wasn't early in the day. They settled on Thursday at 1:30 in the afternoon.

With the help of her GPS, Huber arrived at the front entrance of Ms. Dewitt's apartment complex with five minutes to spare and pulled into one of the visitors' parking spaces. Adjacent to the vehicle entry gate, there was a small pedestrian entrance with a directory.

Huber pushed the button for unit B6 and heard a woman's voice say, "Who is it?"

"R. A. Huber."

"Come on over; second building to your right, ground floor."

A buzzer sounded and Huber pushed the gate open and then walked to building B as directed. The two-story structures were in good repair and the grounds looked well taken care of with manicured lawns, rows of decorative bushes with pinkish-red blossoms, and perennial flower beds. She passed a pool located between buildings A and B. Other than a lone swimmer, she did not cross paths with anyone. People must be at work or school, she presumed.

Before Huber could ring the bell, Jasmine opened the door and said, "Come in. I'm brewing coffee. Want some?"

Huber followed her into the living room and replied, "No thanks, I had lunch a short while ago."

"Mind if I fix myself something?   I haven't had breakfast yet."

"Of course not, go ahead."

Huber had studied Jasmine's face when they greeted one another at the door and now she watched her leave the room. Her facial features were a bit harsh, but she was definitely good-looking with straight, long blond hair and light eyes. She wore a T-shirt and skimpy shorts, showing off a well-proportioned body and legs toned to perfection.

She yelled from the kitchen, "Have a seat!"

The seating arrangement consisted of a sofa and two upholstered chairs placed around a coffee table. Huber sat down on one of the chairs and looked the room over. Besides the sofa group, she observed a bookcase, a large screen TV, and a standing lamp. Several pictures on the walls depicted dogs, and there was a photograph of a horse with a dark-haired woman as its rider. Astonished, Huber gazed at the tame décor. She didn't know what she'd expected, but definitely a racier atmosphere. The place looked also neat, which came as a pleasant surprise.

Jasmine returned, carrying a coffee mug in one hand and a plate with a piece of toast in the other. She placed her breakfast on the coffee table and then flopped herself down onto the sofa.

She said, "Gee, I'm getting popular all of a sudden. You know, like, last week, some fancy lawyer interviewed me for hours, and now I have a private eye paying me a visit." And with a mocking smile she continued, "You know, like, I'm not sure if I should feel honored or be on my guard."

Huber stated, "Neither. Just answer my questions honestly and you have nothing to worry about. By the way, I do appreciate that you agreed to see me."

"No problem. You know, like, I wouldn't be thrilled to talk with anyone early in the day, but as we're having afternoon, I'm fine with it."

Huber thought that interviewing this young woman stood in stark contrast to the tongue-tied Rachel Penrose. Obviously, Jasmine enjoyed talking, and her fast way of speech, with a few "you know, likes" thrown in for good measure, made Huber's head spin.

"I understand that you work as a stripper at Club Marzipan, correct?"

"I prefer the term exotic dancer."

"Fair enough. Club Marzipan is located in North Hollywood, if I'm not mistaken."

"That's right. It's an easy commute from here."

"So you do your exotic dance routines there. What else does your job entail?"

Jasmine swallowed a bite of toast and replied, "I'll do an occasional lap dance, you know, like, if the tip is right, but customers cannot touch."

"How long have you been working at Club Marzipan?"

"Three years. I started at 21 and have seniority status now."

"Did Steven Moretti hire you to come to his house on April 4?"

"Hire me? No, why would he?" Then sudden anger flared up in her eyes and she said, "Let's get one thing straight: I am *not* a hooker."

"I beg your pardon; I've made a wrong assumption."

"Yes, you have."

Then Huber asked, "Where did you first meet Steven Moretti?"

Jasmine had already forgiven Huber her *faux pas* and answered, "He was a regular at Club Marzipan. One night, he waited for me after the club closed and we talked. Then, you know, like, one thing led to another and we've been friends ever since."

"So how long did you know him?"

"At least two years, probably longer."

Giving herself time to think up the next question Huber focused on the pictures on the wall and said, "You obviously like animals."

"Yes, especially dogs. I'd love to keep one, but pets aren't allowed in this apartment complex."

"You have a nice place here; I can imagine that one-bedroom apartments are hard to find."

"Oh, it's a two-bedroom. I couldn't afford it alone and have a roommate." She pointed to the photo of the horse and rider and said, "That's her."

"Your roommate has perfect equestrian posture."

"Horses are all she cares about. You know, like, I hardly ever see her since she has a day job and leaves way before I get up and is asleep when I come home late at night. And on weekends, she usually takes off for some horse ranch or other."

Huber returned to the matter at hand and asked, "So Mr. Moretti visited your club on a regular basis?"

"He used to a long time ago. I don't think I saw him there in the last year and a half."

Huber studied her for a moment and then said, "By being friends with Steven Moretti, did you mean that you saw each other socially?"

Jasmine laughed and replied, "I wouldn't call it socially. You know, like, we didn't exactly have deep, meaningful conversations, and there were no other people involved." She laughed again and continued in her rapid speech, "We hardly talked at all. The truth is, Steven had an overactive sex drive, and when he wanted some extra fun, or if stressed out to the max, he called me and we'd get together. We always met during the day since I work at night."

She looked Huber straight in the eye when she added, "The fun was mutual; I never accepted any money."

"And this went on undetected for over two years?"

"We were careful. That last time in April, his fiancée came home way sooner than expected."

After a pause Huber asked, "Did you ever hope that your relationship with Steven would develop into more?"

"You mean, did I think he could, you know, like, become my boyfriend and maybe even consider marriage?"

"Something to that effect."

Jasmine became grave and stated, "I don't have a college education, but I'm not an idiot. Not in a million years would a man like Steven want to get serious with someone like me. Besides, I wouldn't have wanted *him!* You know, like, he came across as a stud, had tons of money, dressed and talked the big shot, but underneath it all, he was nothing but a calculating jerk."

Huber said, "Thanks for being open with me."

Then she posed her final question, "Do you believe that Rachel is guilty of killing Steven Moretti?"

"Absolutely."

"How can you be so sure? According to my information, you did not know her."

"True, I never met her until that damned Wednesday at the beginning of April, but I wish I could describe the face she made when walking in on us."

"Try."

"She had murder on her mind, is all I can say."

CHAPTER 9

"Feel like a little trip to San Diego?" Huber asked her husband that evening.

"What's in San Diego?"

"Enzo Moretti lives there. He's Steven Moretti's father."

"When did you want to go?"

"I have tomorrow or Saturday in mind, and maybe stay overnight, depending on how things develop."

"I can't. I'm teaching a writers' workshop for a good part of the long weekend."

"Oh, that's right; Memorial Day weekend is coming up. I forgot."

"As usual, you throw things that have nothing to do with your cases out the window!"

"Point taken," she admitted.

He asked, "What did you have in mind when saying you may stay overnight depending on how things developed?"

"What I meant is, talking with Enzo Moretti won't take all day, but he may give me more leads."

"What makes you think that the victim's father would want to see you at all?"

"I've already talked with him on the phone. He said that he doubted he could help me, but that I should feel free to drop by Cucina di Enzo in Little Italy where he eats lunch every day."

"How do you do it?"

"Do what?"

"Getting the most unlikely people to agree to giving you an interview."

"I've had my share of rejections; I just never mention them." And after a pause she said, "I guess I'll drive to San Diego by myself. Andi was willing to cancel plans she'd made with her boyfriend, but I wouldn't hear of it."

"So you didn't even pick me as your first choice," Peter said mockingly. "Did Andi tell you more about that boyfriend of hers?"

"A little. His name is Bo and he owns a small construction company; just him and two or three employees. I would normally not inquire about a person's age, but since she had mentioned that he reminded her of her daddy, I did. He is 37 and originally from South Carolina."

Peter stated, "That doesn't make him as old as her father would be if alive, but still, 15 years is a big difference. The man must have a past."

"One would think so."

"I hope that doesn't mean he carries lots of baggage. I'd like to meet him. Let's have them over for dinner one day soon."

"I'll suggest it next time I talk with Andi," she replied.

CHAPTER 10

Antoinette LeJeune, known to her friends as Andi, had been content with her life before Bo stepped into it. She was born and raised in New Orleans, Louisiana, where Daddy owned a small bar in the French Quarter. Momma died giving birth to her, so Daddy brought her up on his own. Her childhood had been happy, with Daddy teaching her how to play the fiddle, dance the Cajun Waltz, fish, ride the Harley, load, shoot, and take care of a gun. He had also instructed her in cooking Cajun meals, such as gumbo and jambalaya.

A mere high school senior when Daddy died of liver disease, Andi waited until after graduation before selling his bar and estate, and then rode west to California on her Harley-Davidson. There had also been life insurance and some savings, and Daddy had regularly paid into her college fund. Her inheritance and occasional sleuthing jobs she helped R. A. Huber with enabled Andi to stay afloat.

At the moment, she sat in a lecture hall at UCLA, trying to pay attention to a psychology lecture. Clad in her typical outfit of jeans, black leather jacket, and cowboy boots, she straightened up, tossed her wavy, auburn hair over her shoulders, and focused mischievous green eyes on the lecturer. It was no use. As the professor introduced the class to the theories of Sigmund Freud, her mind wandered and she thought back to that first encounter with Mrs. Huber.

She had been in the Pasadena neighborhood and saw the shingle, *R. A. Huber, Private Detective,* in front of an office. On a whim, she had gone inside and asked Mrs. Huber for work which had led to her first job at *Optimum House* a few months later. That was four years ago when she'd been a kid of 18. Meanwhile, she had earned her associate degree of art from Pasadena City College and now worked toward her bachelor's at UCLA. In those four years, Mrs. Huber had taught her a lot about the sleuthing business; she felt proud and tickled pink to be part of it.

One of her boss's favorite pieces of advice popped into her mind: "It is important to keep body and mind agile in our line of work." Mrs. Huber sure practiced what she preached by working out in the gym on a regular basis and stimulating her brain with Chess, Go, Sudoku, and the like. Andi was aware that each additional job her boss included her in brought new life experiences. It also exposed her to unforeseen dangers, which accounted for a good part of her attraction to the job. The young woman not only admired and held Huber as her mentor but had grown fond of her.

The professor's long-winded words briefly reached her ears "… values and evolutionary basis of unconscious processing …" before she returned to her musing. Yes, life had been good before Bo, but now it has turned out even better! He amounted to everything she valued in a man; he was smart, courageous, strong, humorous, caring, and a Southerner riding a Harley to boot. That he also was tall with rugged good looks, sandy hair, and penetrating gray eyes was the icing on the cake. Andi believed that for the first time in her life she had found true love.

They had so much fun getting to know each other while riding their bikes on back roads, playing Frisbee golf, going to the movies, or just talking. Tonight, Bo would take her out to *The Alligator*, a Cajun restaurant that provided live music and dance on Friday nights.

Laughter erupted among students around her. She was clueless of what had triggered the outburst. The professor must have made a joke, she deduced. Holy Krewe! His lecture is nearly over, she thought. About time I start listenin' or I'll flunk the course.

CHAPTER 11

Little Italy is located at the northwest end of Downtown San Diego and borders Laurel Street to the north, Ash Street to the south, Interstate 5 to the east, and the San Diego Bay to the west. Historically, the district was home to Italian fishermen and their families making a living from tuna and other deep-sea commercial fishing. Since the late 1990s, the area went through gentrification. Its main street, India Street, now boasts of public art plazas, galleries, antique stores, and numerous restaurants with outdoor seating. It has become an active neighborhood, offering frequent festivals and events, including a weekly farmers market.

On Friday, May 25, Enzo Moretti sat at his usual table at Cucina di Enzo, eating lunch, as he had done most every day since the passing of his wife, Giuseppa. With his appetite diminishing daily, he could only manage a mixed green salad. Sometimes an old neighborhood friend or two would join him, but on that Friday he ate alone. A steady flow of patrons entered the restaurant, but lost in thought, he did not seem to notice any activity around him.

He had never been one to wallow in self-pity, yet at that moment he longed desperately for an end to his life. When diagnosed with advanced pancreatic cancer in February, he had prayed to God that he might live long enough to see Steven get married. Now he wished he could have died before that horrible day on April 8. Keeping up a good attitude got harder with each day.

In happier times, he used to take pride and be involved in all the Little Italy annual events, like the Art Walk, where thousands of people came to buy articles of art, or the *Gran Fondo,* with bicycle riders from all over the world participating in a 100-mile ride that started under the Little Italy landmark sign. Just last weekend – as was customary in the month of May – Little Italy celebrated the Sicilian Festival, featuring Italian and Sicilian entertainment, old world vendors, and Sicilian cuisine. And in September, he used to enjoy the Labor Day Stickball Tournaments, where several stickball leagues played on the streets of Little Italy.

The December Christmas Village and Tree Lighting event had been Giuseppa's favorite, with Santa Claus riding in on Little Italy's Fire Engine, kicking off the festivities with music, shopping, and fizzy snowflakes for the kids. And not all that long ago, he had enjoyed participating in their weekly farmers market. He sighed and thought, I've lost interest in all of it. Now I just wait for the merciful day I'm permitted to die.

The old gentleman had long finished his salad and Hanna, the waitress, pulled him out of his daydream by asking, "Espresso, Mr. Moretti?"

"Might as well," he answered, "I'm waiting for someone."

CHAPTER 12

Written in parenthesis next to Enzo Moretti's name on the list Huber received from David Wachterman's secretary was "has terminal cancer." Consequently, she expected to meet a sick man. When she came face to face with him on that Friday afternoon, his appearance nonetheless jolted her. The frail hunched-forward figure with a few white hairs sticking out of his bold head who stood up to greet her seemed close to death. To her astonishment, she found his handshake firm and his brown eyes steady.

He said, "Are you hungry?"

"I've stopped for lunch on my drive over; thanks for asking."

"Espresso or Cappuccino, then?"

"An espresso sounds lovely," Huber said, "I appreciate your hospitality."

"Comes with the territory," he replied.

Past two o'clock, the lunch crowd started to taper off. Moretti signaled Hanna over and said, "An espresso for the lady, please."

Huber studied him carefully once more. Then she smiled and said, "You surprise me, Mr. Moretti. I expected an angry, maybe even hostile man, and here you are, saddened, but extremely kind."

"Believe me, my first reaction to Steven's murder was anger. I can't keep it up anymore now; being enraged takes too much energy out of me."

"I know that you are ill. I'm sorry."

"Please, no sympathy. I hate it when people feel sorry for me."

Huber looked around the restaurant and remarked, "I've dined in Cucina di Enzo's in Pasadena and also Glendale. The general décor is the same," and pointing to the hand-painted mural of an Italian fishing village covering the entire length of one wall, she continued, "but this is unique."

"Yes, it is. The artist is long dead, but the mural has lasted 40 years, ever since I opened the *Cucina* with the help of my parents."

"So your folks provided the financing?"

"Not at all! At only 24, I convinced a local banker to give me a loan for starting the restaurant. At the time California's tuna industry was declining, and Dad, a fisherman, hardly could make ends meet. So lucky for me, he helped with the cooking and Mom with the serving."

He went on, "A few years later, I married my Giuseppa, who also chipped in. My Cucina di Enzo soon became one of the first fine dining restaurants in the neighborhood and did well. By the time Steven was born, I could afford to hire help. And a good thing too, since my parents were getting old and ready to retire."

Huber said, "So out of your original Cucina di Enzo here in San Diego evolved a chain restaurant business."

"Not for a long time. Steven had the idea of opening more restaurants, and I was against it in the beginning. I would've been perfectly content with what I had here."

He sighed and said, "The boys got an education; Steven majored in business and Keith went to a Chef's College. I thought that they'd eventually take over my restaurant, but Steven had bigger plans. I had put some money aside over the years and he talked me into opening a second Cucina di Enzo in Del Mar. He had a good business sense and it prospered. Then one thing led to another and we ended up with Cucina di Enzo, Incorporated, with privately owned stock. Steven had even bigger plans with franchises and the whole caboodle. Not wanting to compromise quality of food and a loyal customer base, I put my foot down and resisted franchising the company or going public. To date, we have a dozen restaurants scattered all over Southern California, more than plenty, in my opinion."

Huber saw misery in his brown eyes when he stated, "I am president and was co-owner with Steven as CEO. Now I am the sole owner. What good is fortune and success to me? I buried a wife and two kids, and my only living son is far off at sea. I don't even have any grandkids."

Perplexed, Huber asked, "You had three children?"

"Yes, we did. Steven, Keith, and Jennifer. We gave them American names, which doesn't mean that Giuseppa and I weren't proud of our Italian heritage, but our home is here."

"May I ask what happened to your wife and Jennifer?"

"Giuseppa had a massive stroke three years ago, and our sweet Jennifer got caught in a riptide and drowned."

"That's horrible!"

"It happened 17 years ago when she was only 13. She would've turned 30 next month. Giuseppa never completely recovered. It isn't normal to see one's children go first. I'm glad she was spared the killing of Steven."

Focused on the man's story, Huber had failed to notice that Hanna served her espresso minutes ago. She saw it sitting in front of her now and took a couple of sips before letting the brew get totally cold.

Then she said, "If it's not too painful, tell me about Steven."

"Didn't they give you the details?"

"I don't mean what happened to him recently. I'd like to know what kind of person he was."

After a pause he replied, "Things always came easy to Steven. He managed to get top grades at school without putting much effort into his studies, and also excelled as an athlete. He had a quick mind and knew how to shape everything in life to his advantage. As an adult, he became a successful businessman. Whatever he touched turned to gold. Mind you, he was no angel, and women were his downfall. I hate to say it, but womanizing in the worst degree became a way of life with him. He made me happy by getting engaged to Rachel and finally seemed to settle down."

"Did you like her?"

He sighed again and replied, "I did, and thought her to be good for Steven, keeping him on the right track. It goes to show you how wrong I was."

"So you believe that Rachel is guilty?"

"I know that lawyer of hers hired you to find another possible suspect, but I don't see how you can come up with one since all the evidence points to her."

Huber did not correct him as to who paid for her services and asked, "When did you last see Steven?"

He thought about it for a moment and then said, "Must have been at the beginning of January when we went to his housewarming. No, wait - - I saw him later, in February, at the last board meeting I went to."

"When you said 'we went to his housewarming,' who went with you?"

"My son Keith came home for the holidays and stayed with me until the middle of January. We drove to La Cañada Flintridge together. As a matter of fact, the return trip home was a pain. We happened to be on the road during a police car chase. They closed the 5 Freeway, making us take surface streets all the way from San Clemente. All traffic got redirected to the same detour streets. Especially driving through the small town of Kurtsbad slowed us to a snail pace. What would normally be a two-and-a-half hour drive took nearly four hours." He shook his head and remarked, "Driving has become stressful. I gave it up and donated the car to charity the other day."

"A wise decision, I'm sure." And stirring the conversation back to her objective, she said, "You said earlier that Keith is at sea. Is he taking a cruise?"

"Keith's on a cruise liner, but not as a guest. He's the executive chef on board."

"I see. So being part of the family business is not his cup of tea?" She realized her slip-up as soon as the words were out and covered her mouth.

Enzo Moretti didn't blink an eye and answered, "Keith *was* in it and in charge of the Irvine restaurant, but he didn't see eye to eye with Steven on several business matters. The two got into a big fight at a board meeting about two-and-a-half years ago, and Keith wanted out. After we settled on his share and paid him off, having no more ties to Cucina di Enzo, he left California."

"Where did you stand in their dispute?"

With a sad shrug of the shoulder he replied, "I kept out of it, not wanting to take sides. To tell the truth, some of the discussions at the board meetings are over my head. I don't attend regularly, even though I'm the president."

"I take it that your sons had long called a truce, since Keith went to Steven's housewarming party."

"It took Keith a while, but yes, they made up. Their opinions may have differed in business, but they were still brothers."

Huber looked around the restaurant, taking time to think up more lines of questioning. At nearly 3:30 in the afternoon, the place had emptied except for a couple seated at the far end. When she looked back at her companion, he seemed near exhaustion. This talk is draining him, she thought. I'd better wrap it up soon.

She asked, "Who is taking Steven's place as CEO?"

"That'd be Marco Valente, a distant relative."

"I have him on my list of people to talk with." And she inquired, "Did Steven make a will?"

"I doubt it. The young think they're invincible."

"But you made one?"

"Yes, I made a living trust and will, but its content is hardly any of your business."

I had that coming, Huber thought. Then she asked, "Do you know if Steven kept in contact with anyone from his childhood?"

"He was in touch with Bart Trimboli. They practically grew up together."

"Do you happen to know where Bart Trimboli is now?"

"Sure, he lives 14 miles south of here in Imperial Beach and even comes to see me once in a while." Taking his iPhone out of his trouser pocket, he checked Bart's number and gave it to her, saying, "Call him in the evening after he gets home from work. He's a systems analyst at a high-tech company here in town."

Huber said, "Thanks, and thank you so much for the interview. I kept you a long time. May I give you a ride home?"

"I live nearby and so far have made it on my own two feet every day."

As Huber pulled her wallet out of her purse, Enzo Moretti said, "Don't be silly, the espresso is on the house."

She got up, then bent down and spontaneously gave him a big hug. Without another word she turned on her heels and quickly left his establishment.

CHAPTER 13

Huber checked into a hotel in San Diego's Gaslamp District, changed into comfortable walking shoes, and then went for a stroll. Whenever she and Peter happened to be here, they made sure to visit that historic part of Downtown San Diego. She started at Broadway and walked the approximately ten blocks along 5th Avenue down to Harbor Drive. As she went along storefronts, restaurants, bars, and clubs while keeping pace with numerous tourists, she could not get frail, sad Mr. Moretti out of her mind. Mentally, she made a solemn vow to the old gentleman: *I will seek justice for your son's murder, no matter who did it!*

Near the bay, she strode parallel with the Convention Center, then along the Marina, all the way to Seaport Village. By the time she arrived at the car-free environment of the idyllic village with winding paths connecting its shops, galleries and restaurants, Huber needed a rest. Also ready for dinner, she found a lovely place with waterfront outdoor seating. She ordered grilled sea bass, her motto being when near the ocean, eat fish. She hoped for a local catch, not one imported from China. Her choice ended up being delicious, no matter where it came from.

Before walking all the way back to her hotel she called Bart Trimboli, who agreed to be interviewed at his house the next day, Saturday.

Back in her hotel room, Huber talked with Peter, who said, "Hearing from you this late means you're not on the way home?"

"Right, I'm spending the night.   How did your workshop go?"

"Can't complain.   There wasn't a big turnout, but the folks who attended were interested and paid attention. At the end, we had a lively question-and-answer discussion. A greater number of people signed up for tomorrow's session, so it should be even more rewarding."

She asked, "Did you find something to eat?"

"I'm not completely helpless, you know!   I made myself a salad and cheese omelet. And what did you have for dinner?"

"I walked to Seaport Village and had sea bass."

"In that case, you got the better end of the stick."

Then he asked, "Did you learn anything useful by interviewing Steven Moretti's father?"

"To my surprise, he was eager to tell a lot of stuff. Some of it is sad.   It remains to be seen which of the things are useful to me and which are irrelevant. At this point, I'm just gathering information."

"Feel like unburdening?"

"I thought you'd never ask!" she said, and told Enzo Moretti's gloomy tale.

When she came to the end Peter said, "Poor guy got hit hard from all sides. Approximately how old do you think he is?"

"He's 64, but looks a lot older, which is hardly astonishing, considering his illness and the emotional suffering he's going through."

"Regula! I can't believe you asked the man his age."

"Surely not; it was child's play to figure out. He told me that he opened the original Cucina di Enzo 40 years ago at the age of 24."

Then Peter said, "So even his own father knew that Steven was a philanderer."

"Yes, and he wasn't pleased about it. He hoped that Rachel would keep him on the right track. Those were *his* words, by the way."

"Did he say whether his other son was married?"

"No, and I didn't ask. The fact that he's chef on an ocean liner makes me guess the man is single. It would have to be a long-distance marriage, unless his spouse happened to also be employed on the ship."

"So Regula, since you're not coming home yet, I take it you'll interview that longtime friend of Steven's tomorrow?"

"Correct. I made an appointment to see him at 10 o'clock in the morning at his home in Imperial Beach."

"That's near the Mexican border, I believe." And he asked, "What are you expecting to learn from this boyhood friend of Steven Moretti?"

"I have no idea. If the talk with him results in my obtaining a lead or any other useful information, I'll be ecstatic, and if not, I'll get to visit Imperial Beach and gain a new geographical experience."

"Just don't wander off too far south!" he joked. "What else is on your agenda in San Diego?"

She replied, "Nothing more. If you were here, I'd suggest we go to SeaWorld or the Zoo, but since I'm alone, I'll head home after seeing Bart Trimboli. At what time is your Saturday workshop over?"

"It officially goes until four, but these events always run into overtime. I should get home no later than six."

"In that case, I'll be in no big rush on my return drive and take Pacific Highway for a stretch, maybe as far as Oceanside or San Clemente before hooking up with the 5 Freeway. The landscape along the coast should be beautiful at this time of year, and I love the feel of the little towns on that route. But don't worry, I'll be back in plenty of time to cook us dinner."

"Attagirl!"

CHAPTER 14

Bart Trimboli's house was located only a few short blocks from the beach. Huber arrived promptly at 10 o'clock, and while walking to the front door of the single-story bungalow, heard a baby cry. She rang the bell, which prompted a woman from within to yell, "Bart! Get the front door; I'm busy."

Huber waited at least a minute before someone opened the door. Then she faced Mrs. Trimboli standing at the threshold, holding a five-month-old baby girl in her arms that had stopped crying, but now on eyeing Huber started up again. As if on command, another baby began to bawl somewhere in the house.

Mrs. Trimboli said, "It never fails; when one cries, the other joins in. They must be synchronized." She studied Huber and seemed taken aback, asking, "You're the investigator?"

"Correct, I'm R. A. Huber."

She didn't introduce herself but turned around and vanished into the interior, calling out, "Bart, it's for you!"

Huber still stood at the open door, unsure if welcome to step inside. One of the babies had stopped wailing and the other's cry had turned into a whimper.

A man with a toddler in tow finally showed up and said, "You must be Mrs. Huber. I'm Bart. Come in, please."

They shook hands and Huber said, "If this is a bad time, I can come back later."

He laughed and said, "It's always like this. The twins are fussy - - we're sure they're teething - - and Junior here is getting toilet trained."

"I can see what keeps you and your wife from boredom," she replied with a chuckle of her own and followed him into the living room.

The room looked like true "living." Other than a sofa pushed against a wall, the furnishings were strictly kiddyland. There was a playpen in the center, flanked by baby-swings, jumpers and bouncers. At the far end of the room stood a toy chest, and next to it a rocking horse. Huber and Bart sat down on the sofa, and the little boy ran over to the horse, climbed on it, and started rocking, yelling, "Giddyup, giddyup!"

Huber said, "Thanks for seeing me on short notice. I'm well aware that I'm butting in on your family on this Memorial Day weekend."

"To be honest, if not for Papa Moretti, I'd have avoided talking with you."

"I don't understand."

"He called me yesterday before you did and said I should see the nice lady detective."

"That is truly generous of him. I've noticed that Mr. Moretti is not bitter, despite his horrible fate."

One of the twins made herself audible again, even though the crying came from the adjacent room. Huber had to raise her voice as she continued, "So you keep in touch with him?"

"He's always been like a second father to me. I try to make time to visit him, especially now that he's sick."

The toddler had climbed down from his rocking horse and now banged on a xylophone. His dad shouted, "Sorry about all the noise. I'm used to it, but it must be distracting to you."

No kidding! she thought, as he continued, "Even if we'd go into another room, we'd still hear the commotion."

Huber suggested, "How about taking a walk down to the beach?"

"Great idea! Let me tell my wife. I'll be right back."

Huber heard them talk loudly in the next room, trying to drown out the baby's squeals. Mrs. Trimboli didn't sound too happy, but eventually told him to go ahead.

He reappeared and went over to his son, bent down until eye-level with the toddler and said, "I'm going for a walk with the lady."

"Can I come?"

"Not this time. Mommy needs your help with the twins." He kissed him on the forehead, saying, "Be good for Mommy. I'll be back soon."

CHAPTER 15

They did not talk for the first couple of blocks, making Huber grateful. Striding along in her pumps, she barely managed to keep up with the long steps of her tall companion. He suddenly realized it and slowed down. Both enjoyed this typically sunny day at the end of May with a pleasant temperature of 70 degrees. Huber had not seen anyone above the age of 28 on her drive through the beach town or now on their walk.

She said, "Imperial Beach seems to be a young people's community."

"You've got that right," he agreed. "At 33, I feel like a senior citizen! It's about the only town left with affordable housing near the beach this side of the border. On top of that, it's a surfer's paradise."

"Do you surf?"

"I used to, but hardly find time for it anymore."

She remarked, "Your time is pretty much divided between job and family, I can imagine."

"Yep, but it's worth it. I love having a big family."

"Does your wife enjoy the big family bliss too?"

He grinned and replied, "You're a good observer! I'll admit, she feels overwhelmed by the twins at the moment, but things are apt to get better as they grow older. I keep telling her to look on the bright side; they'll always have built-in playmates."

The first thing that caught Huber's eye when they arrived at the Portwood Pier Plaza was the imposing *Surfhenge*: four enormous colored acrylic moldings that looked like giant surfboards stuck in the sand.

She pointed at the Surfhenge monument and said, "This is impressive."

Then she walked over to one of the ten "surfboard" benches resembling different surfboard styles popular through the decades, located about the plaza, and suggested, "Let's sit down."

They had a magnificent view of the pier, the sandy beach, and the ocean beyond. There were scattered sunbathers and a handful of kids in the water who braved the chilly Pacific Ocean. At the picnic area, folks were setting up tables for their feasts. It was not beach season yet; in another month or so, the sandy shore would be crowded with people frolicking on blankets, under umbrellas, playing volleyball, swimming, surfing, and jogging at the water's edge.

Huber said, "I hate to talk about a murder investigation in such an idyllic setting, but I had better start with the interview so you can get back to your family."

"Shoot."

"So Steven Moretti was your childhood friend, and I understand that you practically grew up together. Tell me a bit about that."

"I spent most of my after-school hours hanging out with the Moretti kids, either in the backroom of Cucina di Enzo or on nearby streets, playing ball games or cops and robbers. Sometimes it was just them and me, other times hordes of neighborhood kids joined us."

"What do you mean by backroom?"

"They had this cool storage room behind the restaurant, which also served as our playroom. It had a ping-pong table, dart-set, Fussball table, and a shelf with board games. Papa Moretti made sure we did our homework first, but then we had the run of the place. As an only child, I relished the company of other kids. Steve, in particular, always came up with tons of cool stuff to do."

"I thought his name was Steven."

"His parents called him Steven but for us kids he went by Steve. Even as an adult when he preferred his formal name, I always called him Steve."

"I can understand why you want to have a big family of your own," Huber said. And she asked, "Were you and Steven the same age?"

"No, I fit right in between; with Steve a year older and Keith a year younger. There was also their baby sister Jennifer who was 3 years younger than me."

"So you played with all three?"

"Mostly just the boys and other neighborhood kids. Once in a while Jennifer stuck around, but not too often."

"Because she was younger and a girl?"

"No, because she was musical."

"Musical?"

"Mrs. Moretti drove her all over town to piano, cello, and singing lessons most weekdays."

"I see. Something strikes me as interesting. You call Enzo Moretti 'Papa Moretti,' but you don't refer to his wife as Mamma Moretti. Is there a reason for that?"

He mulled this over and then said, "Funny, I never thought about it. I think that early on, when in 1st or 2nd grade, Mr. Moretti told me to call him Papa Moretti and Mrs. Moretti must have never suggested that I call her anything but Mrs."

Huber asked, "Were the Moretti boys easy to get along with?"

"As long as he called the shots, Steve proved to be a good friend," he replied. "I had no problem with that. He was a born leader and I felt perfectly happy as his follower. Keith had a temper and put up a fight every now and then, but his older brother always ended up the winner in any dispute and we did things *his* way or not at all."

"What kind of a child was Jennifer?"

"What they call 'gifted.' My parents took me to a classical concert once where she played the piano and I heard her practice her vocals. I was into metal and not impressed."

"Did she get along with her brothers?"

"Jennifer admired Steve and pretty much obeyed his orders. She and Keith were close enough in age for fighting occasionally."

A couple of loud seagulls chased one another three feet above their heads and Huber instinctively ducked. Then she followed the birds with her eyes until she no longer heard their screeching and they had vanished from sight beyond the pier.

She said, "Mr. Moretti mentioned that Jennifer drowned 17 years ago. Not wanting to add to his sorrow, I didn't ask him for any details. Do you know what happened?"

His round good-humored face took on a rueful expression as he said, "I was there."

Perplexed, Huber asked, "You saw her drown?"

He nodded, and then told the sad story. "It was the first weekend in July. Steve drove us all to the beach and - -"

"Who is 'us all'?"

"The Moretti kids and me. At 17, Steve had been driving for about a year. I was turning 16 in September, so I didn't have my license yet. Anyhow, we got to the crowded beach and were lucky to find a decent spot to spread our towels. The surf was rough and there were strong rip currents. Not that Steve and I paid any attention; we were too busy being cool and flirting with two girls who sat in the space next to us. Keith and Jennifer got into a major fight. Jennifer suddenly burst into tears and then ran to the water and dove in. As I said, Steve and I were uninterested in her issue, exchanging phone numbers with our newest conquests. A while later, I noticed that Keith had also left us."

Trimboli took a deep breath before he continued, "When I finally looked out to the ocean, I saw them. They were caught in a riptide. Actually, I only saw Keith struggling with something, but at the time I didn't know it was him. Much later, I learned that Jennifer had panicked and consequently pulled him under as well when he came to her rescue. Steve noticed the commotion in the water too and said, 'Somebody is fighting a riptide.' Suddenly I realized that the person was in real trouble and I ran to alert the lifeguard. We still didn't know that the people in the water were Jennifer and Keith."

After a long pause he went on, "The lifeguards saved Keith, but they were too late for Jennifer."

"What a horrible tragedy you had to witness!"

"It's something that stays with me all my life. If we had not tried to pick up those girls and had not been so clueless to what went on in the water, she might have survived. Steve and I were stronger swimmers than Keith. We might have been able to pull her out of the rip current."

"You can't truly know that, so don't blame yourself."

As if he had not heard her, he said "We've never talked about it, but I know that Steve and Keith were also tormented by guilt."

"I can understand that in Steven's case, but Keith tried to rescue his sister and nearly drowned himself. Why would he feel guilty?"

"Because they had a fight right before she ran away from him and into the water."

Huber nodded and said, "In the mind of a fifteen-year-old boy that fact would register guilt." Then she wondered, "What were they fighting about; do you know?"

"I don't remember what triggered the quarrel, but it got pretty intense before she ran off. She shouted that she'd tell on him about his experimenting with drugs."

He looked at his watch, and Huber said, "We're almost done. Let's get to the present. Have you kept up your friendship with Steven and Keith after you all became adults?"

He replied, "We stayed in steady contact during the college years. And later Steve and I tried to get together whenever our schedules allowed. Same goes for Keith. I haven't seen much of Steve in the last two years though, and I saw Keith only once during that time."

"Is that because you're too busy with your family now?"

"That's part of it, but also because Keith is working on a ship and hardly ever comes home. As for Steve - -" he stopped in mid-sentence and then said, "Oh, what the hell, I might as well tell you, my wife couldn't stand him. I had to drag her to his engagement party even though it was held nearby on Coronado Island. And in January, when we were invited to their housewarming, she had a good excuse. The twins were three-week-old infants, so she stayed home and I made the trip alone."

"Do you know why she disliked him?"

"Oh, she made no secret about it and called him a lecherous wolf with no conscience. She said that she felt sorry for Rachel who in her opinion had blinders on and couldn't see beyond his good looks. We argued about him a lot before the murder because she didn't want to attend his wedding."

"What was *your* opinion of the grown man, Steven Moretti?"

"He was still cool in my book. I admit, he had his faults; mainly being addicted to sex, but we were friends and would be to this day, were he alive."

"There is a lot to be said for loyalty," Huber commented. And she asked, "What kind of an adult did his brother turn out to be?"

"Keith has his own demons of addiction to deal with; he's a compulsive gambler, but I heard he's got it under control now."

Getting to her last question she became grave and inquired, "Do you believe that Rachel Penrose is guilty of killing your friend?"

He replied, "To tell the truth, I wouldn't have expected it of her. She seemed so wholesome. Believe me, I've given this a lot of thought and can't logically come up with someone else who could have done it. The only other person with access to the oleander plant in their garden and to Steve's tea is the housekeeper." He gave Huber a rueful smile as he added, "And I doubt whether you, or anyone else, can find a plausible motive for that lady."

Huber got to her feet and shook his hand, saying, "I appreciate the interview. Thank you! Run on home to your wife and kids now. I'm not in a hurry and prefer to take a stroll on the pier before returning to my car."

CHAPTER 16

Bart's wife came out of the nursery and said, "So far so good, the twins are asleep; we may get an hour's peace and quiet for a change."

Bart had put their toddler down for his afternoon nap and sat at the kitchen table, staring at the opposite wall, sipping his after-lunch coffee.

His spouse joined him and said, "What's the matter? Did the investigator woman upset you?"

He shook his head and said, "No, it's just that she asked me about Jennifer's drowning accident."

"I see."

"I shouldn't have gone into details about it, but she was so easy to talk to." He shook his head again and continued, "It's been years since I talked about that day, but it came back to me as if it happened yesterday. Now I can't get the horrific picture of the lifeguards bringing them on shore out of my head; Keith in a coughing fit, and two guys working on Jennifer's lifeless body."

"Quit tormenting yourself. It wasn't your fault. Besides, I doubt that you or anyone else could have saved her. She was too far gone."

"Maybe not, but Steve and I should have tried, instead of flirting with those girls."

"Even if they hadn't been on the scene, you might not have noticed anything wrong in the water until it was too late."

After a pause she asked, "How long ago has it been?"

Without having to do the math he replied, "Seventeen years."

"It is time to let it rest," his wife said with finality.

At that very moment, Huber made her way home and also had Jennifer on her mind. She drove along the coast, barely noticing the beauty of the calm ocean and blue sky stretching before her or the median road divider of bushes with lovely blooming pink flowers while she passed through the small town of Kurtsbad. The loss of such a young, talented daughter and sister must have been enormous for the Moretti family, she mused. And the burden of guilt the three boys lived with must be everlasting.

She gave herself a mental slap on the wrist and thought, stop dwelling on the past, Regula. Concentrate on solving Steven's murder.

CHAPTER 17

On Tuesday, right after the holiday weekend, the Hubers invited Andi and her boyfriend Bo over for dinner at their home in Merida. Already on Monday the weather had turned unfriendly and cold. By Tuesday, the temperature had dropped even lower. The gray sky was a prelude of an imminent storm. R. A. Huber decided to serve a cheese fondue one last time before putting the fondue pot on the back shelf in her cupboard until winter. Her choice of menu was not only appropriate for the chilly weather, but the cozy, leisurely atmosphere that went with such a dish would give them a good chance to chat during the meal.

When the two arrived in the evening, a strong wind blew accompanied by pounding rain. Not having umbrellas, they waited in Bo's pickup truck until the downpour eased a bit and then made a run for it. Andi sprinted ahead of Bo, despite wearing a dress and high heels. Peter greeted them at the door and took their wet coats before showing them into the dining room, while Regula came out of the adjacent kitchen to welcome them.

She gave Andi a hug and said, "You look fantastic in spite of being wet!" And shaking the man's hand, she continued, "I'm happy to meet you, Bo!"

"Nice to meet you too," he replied. "Andi thinks the world of you, Mrs. Huber."

"Please sit down and have some appetizers while I get things under control," she said, and vanished back into the kitchen.

Peter gave Andi an appreciative look over and stated, "It is a rare treat to see you in a skirt!"

"Since I'm not ridin' the Harley tonight, I had no excuse to wear my signature outfit of jeans and leather jacket," she replied with a smirk.

The three sat down at the set table and helped themselves to a variety of veggie toothpick finger foods, like sautéed button mushrooms, artichoke hearts, radishes, asparagus tips in vinaigrette, cherry tomatoes, and pickled beets.

Meanwhile, R. A. Huber tended to things in the kitchen. She had previously coated the shredded Gruyere and Emmenthaler cheese with cornstarch and rubbed the inside of the fondue pot with garlic. She now poured dry white wine into the pot and turned the stove's gas flame to medium. When the wine came to a simmer, she slowly added the cheese mixture, a handful at a time, while constantly stirring in a zigzag pattern to prevent the cheese from seizing, in other words, from separating the wine from the cheese, and balling up. She cooked and stirred until the cheese melted and became creamy. Then she added the final touches of nutmeg, pepper and Kirsch.

She carried the pot with the bubbling fondue to the dining room and set it onto the chafing dish, which Peter had already lit. The platter holding cubes of French bread sat at the ready on the table.

Andi burst out, "I'm tickled pink that you're serving fondue, my favorite Swiss food!"

"I had you *and* the weather in mind!"

Bo commented, "June gloom is hitting a couple of days early this year."

Peter opened a bottle of Sauvignon Blanc and poured it into their goblets. They clanked glasses and cheered, "*Prost!*" before taking the first sip. Then they speared chunks of bread with their forks, dipped them into the fondue, twirled, eased them to their mouths, and enjoyed.

They ate in silence until Bo said, "You whipped up a mighty fine dish, ma'am. I'm obliged!"

His charm was not lost on Huber and she replied, "I'm a sucker for compliments, especially when they're uttered in a Southern drawl."

Peter asked, "You're from South Carolina?"

"Yes, sir, near Charleston."

"How long have you lived in California?"

"Nine years, and I like it fine here."

"You own a construction business, I gather."

"Just a small one; me and a few employees from south of the border. As far as I know, they're legal."

Andi jumped in, "Tell them what you do on weekends."

Bo said, "It's no big deal. I bought myself a house, what you'd call a fixer upper, and I work on fixin' every Saturday and Sunday. I can't live in it yet, but it's shaping up and may be ready to move in by the middle or end of June."

Andi exclaimed, "He tore most of the old house down and is building it up proper. I saw it the other day; the place is gonna turn out gorgeous!"

"How exciting," Huber said. "Where is it?"

"In the Valley, not far from here."

Peter asked Bo, "Where do you live now?"

"In an apartment in Culver City, but my business is located in San Fernando. That's why I bought property close by."

Andi remarked, "He works so hard and still finds time for me!" She eagerly went on, "The weekends are taken up by his house project, but when I don't have late classes, he steals away in the afternoon. We've gone ridin' in the desert, tried out several Frisbee golf courses, hiked in the local mountains, and last Friday night, Bo took me to *The Alligator* for dinner and Cajun dancing."

As she ran out of things to mention, they all concentrated on eating. Bo thought, the Missus seems to like me, but I'm not sure about the man. Since these two people are close to Andi, I need to make a good impression. I should've read one of the man's books so I could compliment him about his writing.

He pulled out of his musing when Andi suddenly continued her repertoire, "We have a lot in common; ridin' the Harleys, of course, and we discovered that we both are fans of old Western movies." Full of enthusiasm, she continued, "And listen to this: Bo even sat at Daddy's bar once, when on a visit to New Orleans. Isn't that the coolest?"

Smiling, Huber remarked, "It's a small world."

"And as he's familiar with my hometown, I didn't have to explain that a Krewe is an organization that parades at Mardi Gras."

When the fondue had dwindled away until they were left with nothing but the crust, Bo said, "That was a mighty fine dinner!"

Peter took his fork and, scraping out the layers of cooked-on cheese in the pot, mentioned, "That's the best of the entire fondue, right at the bottom." And with the other hand he made a halting gesture toward his spouse. "Don't even say it!"

Andi and Bo looked astonished and then Andi asked, "What were you going to say, boss?"

Peter answered for her and stated, "Not to be such a glutton and leave some crust for her." And as he turned the fondue pot towards his wife who started poking at the brown residue, he said, "Being married as long as we are, we know each other's mind." And to Bo, "Have you ever been married?"

Bo was taken off guard for a couple of seconds and then answered, "Can't say that I have." With an awkward grin, he explained, "If truth be told, I never found the right woman to tie the knot with." And taking Andi's hand in his continued, "That's gonna change now."

Andi looked him in the eye and blushed.

CHAPTER 18

After coffee and dessert Andi insisted on helping Huber clean up. The two carried trays with dirty dishes to the kitchen and left the men to themselves.

The minute they shut the door behind them, Andi asked, "And? Do you like him?"

"He's handsome and has a lot of Southern charm."

"Sure thing, but do you *like* him?"

"He seems nice; I hardly know him, though."

"Admit it, boss, it bugs you that he's older."

"That in itself is not the issue. I can see that you are in love and I'm happy for you."

"But?"

"You said that Bo reminds you of your father, and maybe ..."

Andi interrupted, "He doesn't look like Daddy, if that's what's bothering you. He's taller than Daddy was and they have different coloring. Only his mannerism is what's similar to Daddy's."

"I just don't want you to get hurt."

"Why would I get hurt?"

Huber did not respond, and Andi finally said, "Oh, I get it. You reckon if it doesn't work out, I'll fall apart. Damn it! I'm a grown woman and can take care of myself."

They rinsed and stacked the plates and coffee cups into the dishwasher. Huber looked out the window. Dusk had long turned into night, making it pitch-dark outside. The rain came down sideways and pelted the glass in a relentless stream.

She said, "I think it's getting worse out there. I hope it'll ease by the time you leave."

Andi had no interest in the weather and said, "I'm sorry about not showing up for target shooting practice; I plumb forgot. I remembered too late and knew you'd already be on your way home."

"Don't worry about it; you've been preoccupied with Bo lately."

"That's no excuse. I went a few days later to make up for it, but I'm still ashamed."

The wine glasses and fondue forks had to be hand washed, so Huber washed and Andi dried.

Andi asked, "How's the new case coming along?"

"It is too early to form a clear picture, but I'll fill you in on the interviews I had in San Diego." And she enlightened her assistant with what she had learned from Enzo Moretti and Bart Trimboli.

As Huber retold the part about Mr. Moretti losing his daughter in the drowning accident, Andi said, "That poor old man! But like Daddy used to say, *le bon Dieu* only dishes out what we can handle."

At the end of her boss's narrative Andi mulled the information over and then said, "That guy Bart is right. I can't see anyone else having a motive to kill Steven other than Rachel, at least not any of the people you've talked to so far. Even that hooker had nothing to gain by murdering him."

"Stripper, not hooker," Huber corrected. "Jasmine made certain I understood the difference."

"On the other hand, folks seem surprised that Rachel had done the murder. What's your take on it?"

"Well Andi, in a court of law a person is innocent until proven guilty. By now you should know that for the purpose of my investigations, I turn the phrase around."

"Sure thing, I know it word for word: Everyone is a suspect until proven otherwise."

"Exactly!"

"You reckon Steven had a deep, dark secret that his fiancée was about to get wise to shortly before their wedding and he killed himself?"

"I appreciate your sense of imagination and drama, but suicide is a bit farfetched. There are plenty of faster and less painful ways to end one's own life than this kind of poisoning. Besides, if that were his plan, why call 911 and take the chance of being saved?"

"I see your point, boss." And she asked, "What's your next move?"

"I'll interview several board of directors and Rufina Ramos, the housekeeper, and hopefully get some information I can sink my teeth into."

"What about Steven's brother? Does he get off his ship someday soon so you can question him?"

"I'll have to find out about that."

"Want me to tackle the housekeeper? I can do it evenings."

"She lives closer to me, and don't you have to study for finals?"

"Yes, ma'am."

As Andi placed the last goblet on the cupboard shelf, Huber said, "I'm letting the fondue pot soak, so we're done. Let's get back to the men."

An hour later, while Peter and Regula relaxed in the living room, the latter said, "The fondue turned out well.

As you know, I don't take that for granted ever since the time the cheese separated." And she asked, "Did you enjoy the meal and company?"

"The fondue tasted perfect and Andi looked stunning. I believe this was only the second time I saw her in a dress. As for Bo, I don't know what to say."

"What did you talk about while Andi and I washed up?"

"Oh, mostly construction in general, and the remodeling of his house in particular. He seems to have a wide range of knowledge in the field - - from foundation to roofing, and everything in between. He also inquired about the books I write, but I think he did so just to make conversation and doubt he had any true interest in my writing. And what did you two discuss in the kitchen?"

"I kept her up to date on the current job, and of course we chatted about Bo. It is important to her that I like him. Doubtless you've noticed that there is a strong physical attraction between them."

Peter asked, "You think their relationship is already advanced?"

"If you mean, are they sexually involved, the answer is yes."

"Don't tell me you asked her!"

"I didn't have to; I know." Then she said, "What do you think of him as a man, or rather, as Andi's boyfriend?"

"I don't trust him."

"Those are strong words, Peter. Can you back them up with a reason?"

"No, it's just my gut feeling."

CHAPTER 19

Huber's next few days were taken up by general maintenance, consisting of appointments for haircut, manicure/pedicure, dental hygienist and her annual physical. She smiled to herself as she left the doctor's examining room on Friday, recalling his remark. He had been her physician for decades and joked, "If all my patients were like you, showing up only once a year with a clean bill of health, I'd be out of business!"

To stay on the subject of doctors, when she got back to her office on that Friday afternoon, Jonathan Lighthart called inquiring about her progress.

She said, "Dr. Lighthart, rest assured that I'm investigating Rachel's case to the best of my ability. I never disclose my opinion or findings until I'm 100% sure of the truth. To date, I haven't even seen half the people I'm planning to talk to."

"I apologize," he replied, "I guess I'm overanxious, but the trial is in August and today we have the 1st of June already."

"I understand your concern but am positive that I can get a lot accomplished between now and then."

He asked, "Have you talked to Rachel?"

"I have. She doesn't make my task easy with her passive attitude."

"So she's still docile. I was afraid of that."

Huber said, "For her own good, I hope that she snaps out of it soon."

"I shouldn't have bothered you. Do you need another advance fee?"

"That's not necessary. I'm fine for the moment. I'll send you a detailed invoice soon. By the way, no one knows of your involvement and I didn't even have to dodge any questions. Rachel thinks her parents hired me, and the victim's father assumes that I work for her lawyer."

"I appreciate that."

Huber stated, "I want you to be clear on something, Doctor. Just because you don't hear from me on a regular basis doesn't mean that I'm neglecting Rachel's case."

After they ended the call, Jonathan Lighthart stared at the phone for a long time, thinking, I wonder if the woman is any good. She may have been on top of things in her investigation of the murders at Optimum House, but this is different. Can she catch the real killer given the strong allegation against Rachel?

CHAPTER 20

Rufina Ramos and her family lived in an apartment in Glendale. After dinner on Monday evening, she sat on their sofa with her feet up, relaxing after a hard day's work of cleaning someone else's home. Her husband had just left for the night shift at a local supermarket where he worked as a meat cutter. Their sixteen-year-old daughter banged dishes around in the kitchen, being less than pleased with the chore of cleaning up, and her younger brother had vanished into his room with orders to get homework done.

At 37, Rufina was still a pretty woman with long dark hair pulled into a bun, a bronze complexion that needed no make-up, and big brown eyes. She had married early and gave birth to her firstborn son a year later. He now attended college, which made her feel proud. All their hard work and saving every extra penny proved worth it; they'd reached their goal of being able to give him an education. Whether there'd be any money left for his siblings when their time came was another matter. As always, Rufina and her husband took one day at a time.

When Huber arrived at 7:30 in the evening, Rufina greeted her at the door and ushered her into the kitchen, asking, "Would you like something to drink?"

"No, thank you. This won't take long," Huber replied.

They each pulled up a chair to the kitchen table and Rufina said, "I don't understand. When you called, you said that you were a detective looking into the murder of Mr. Moretti. I already talked to somebody else from the police, and as far as I know, Ms. Penrose got arrested."

"I'm a private investigator, not affiliated with the authorities. And you are right; Rachel Penrose was arrested for Steven Moretti's murder. Someone does not believe her to be guilty and hired me to look into the matter. In other words, I'm conducting my investigation with the idea that she may be innocent."

"I get it now. You're trying to find another murderer. But I don't know anything about it. I wasn't even there when he died."

"I'm aware of that," Huber said, "I'm just going to ask some general questions about Steven Moretti's household. Some of my inquiry may be repetitive of what the police already covered."

Rufina's daughter tried to sneak by them and had already made it to the door when her mom called out to her, "Where do you think you're going, young lady?"

"Just down the street to see Trish."

"It's dark already; you're not going out anymore on a school night. You know the rule."

Reluctantly the teen turned around, rolling her eyes. Then she obediently went back to her room, and Rufina yelled after her, "And no more texting or talking on the phone until your homework is done." She turned back to Huber and said, "Sorry about that."

"No problem. I remember the time when my kids were teenagers." Then she said, "I detect a slight accent. Where are you originally from?"

"My parents came over from Brazil when I was twelve, but we only spoke Portuguese at home. That's why I still have an accent."

"Does your husband also have a Brazilian background?"

"No, he is second-generation Mexican with no accent. Neither of us went to college. That's why we're so strict with the kids. We want them to have a better life." And she asked, "Are you German?"

"I'm from Switzerland and have tried to get rid of my accent ever since I got here at the age of twenty." And easing into the questioning, she said, "Now, Mrs. Ramos, how long were you employed as Steven Moretti's housekeeper?"

"Oh, about four years."

"That surprises me. I heard that he had a housewarming at the beginning of this year. People usually don't wait that long with such an event after purchasing a house."

"I already cleaned his condominium in Glendale before he bought the house in La Cañada."

"That clarifies the matter for me. When did he move to the La Cañada property?"

"I think last August or September, and soon afterward he got engaged and Ms. Penrose moved in."

"I learned that they gave an engagement party. Did they also hold that at his house?"

"No, it was a big to-do; they rented a hotel hall on Coronado Island near San Diego."

"What about the housewarming in January? Did you help them with that?"

"They didn't need me. Mr. Moretti hired a catering company."

Then Huber said, "Working for Mr. Moretti for four years, you must have known him well."

"Not really, I didn't see him often. I cleaned his place every Thursday and got there around 10:00 in the morning when he'd already left for work."

"Was he a nice man?"

She shrugged and said, "None of my business what kind of man he was. He paid me well. That's why I agreed to follow him to La Cañada, even though I had to walk far from the bus station to his house."

"You don't drive?"

"We only have one car. My husband dropped me off whenever he had the night shift, but if he worked days, I took the bus."

Huber smiled and remarked, "I hope that all your other employers live in Glendale."

"Most of 'em do."

"What did your job as housekeeper at the Moretti residence entail?"

"I cleaned the entire house, except windows - - I don't do windows - - going from room to room. You know, kitchen and bathrooms, including mopping floors, and vacuuming, dusting, and polishing furniture in the rest of the house." She added, "I had a routine, but if I saw extra work, like dishes in the sink, cobwebs on ceilings, or smudges on walls, I took care of it."

"You've got a tiring job."

"Hard work doesn't bother me. I'm healthy and strong."

"What did you think of Rachel Penrose?"

"I didn't see her much either, but she was nice. That's why I thought there must be a mistake when I first heard that she - -" Rufina stopped abruptly.

"You had a hard time believing that she murdered Mr. Moretti?"

She nodded.

Huber said, "I assume you know how he died."

"Yes, he drank poisoned tea, so I'm told."

"Naturally, I am interested in that tea. I understand that Mr. Moretti habitually drank tea made from loose tea leaves."

"That's right. It came from England, from Tea Brewer."

"Tea Brewer is the company that shipped the tea?"

"Right."

"I take it that he was a tea connoisseur?"

"I don't think so, but at one time he had an English girlfriend who drank it. I guess he liked the stuff and switched from coffee to tea."

"When was that?"

"Oh, a long time ago."

"Did you brew the tea for him?"

"Oh no, he always fixed it himself, using an infuser."

"You knew where he kept it, though?"

Rufina's Latin temper suddenly flared up and she exclaimed, "Don't you dare accuse me of poisoning his tea. Why would I want to kill Mr. Moretti? Just the opposite, I lost a good job!"

Huber calmed her down and said, "I'm suggesting no such thing. I just need information as to where he kept the loose tea."

"He had it in a canister on the kitchen counter and added new tea leaves whenever he ran low."

Huber asked, "Do I understand this correctly; he received new tea shipments from England on a regular basis?"

"That's right."

"Do you have any idea when he received the last one?"

"The mailman handed the package to me on a day I worked there."

"When?"

"Thursday, March 29."

"How can you be sure of the date?"

"The police asked me the same question, and at the time I had it still fresh in my mind."

Huber took a small calendar out of her purse and, checking the date, murmured to herself, "That was the week before Rachel moved out of his house."

Then she addressed the housekeeper again and said, "On the following Thursday, April 5, you were also cleaning the Moretti house when Ms. Penrose collected her belongings. Correct?"

"That's right."

Loud music suddenly sounded from one of the back rooms, and Rufina shouted, "Turn it down, Carlos!" Then she gave Huber an apologetic smile.

"Tell me about that day, please."

She recalled, "Ms. Penrose came in the afternoon to get her things. With their wedding only ten days away and seeing the suitcases, I said, 'Are you packing early for your honeymoon?' She laughed hysterically, almost an inhuman laugh, and said, 'That's very funny!' Then she pulled herself together and told me about what happened the day before and that she just came to get her clothes and other stuff. I asked if she needed help, but she preferred doing it alone, which I understood."

"Did she go to the backyard?"

"Yes. I had gone back to cleaning and saw her from the window of an upstairs room digging out her herbs and carefully packing each plant."

"Did the oleander bush stand close to the herb garden?"

"No, it was at the other end of the yard."

"Did she go near it?"

"I only watched her for a short time before continuing my vacuuming." And with a tone of finality in her voice she stated, "Like I told the police, I saw her by the herb garden and nowhere else."

"Who left the house first?"

"She only stayed for about an hour. I wasn't done cleaning when she left. It's a big house."

"Did she go into the kitchen?"

"I don't know. When she told me she didn't want any help, I left her alone and minded my own business."

"How would you describe Rachel Penrose's disposition on that day?"

"What do you mean?"

"Was she angry, sad and devastated, in a rage?"

"All of that, I think, but she concentrated on gathering her stuff as quickly as possible so she could get out of there."

"Did you talk some more?"

"Not much. When ready to go, she said good-bye and that she'd left her house key in the foyer. I told her that I was sorry for what happened and wished her well."

Huber said, "Coming back to Steven Moretti, do you think he had any enemies?"

"Probably, but I wouldn't know who they are. As I told you before, I hardly knew him."

"Who had a key to the house besides Mr. Moretti, Ms. Penrose, and yourself?"

"Nobody, I think." And she added, "I never asked."

"What is the name of Mr. Moretti's former girlfriend, do you know?"

"Which one? He had lots of them."

"I meant the woman from England."

Rufina reflected for a moment and then replied, "I can't remember her name."

"What can you tell me about Jasmine Dewitt?"

"Should I know her? Oh, wait. - - Is that the stripper?"

"Correct. Did you ever hear of her before?"

"I don't think so."

The idea which Andi had thrown in entered Huber's mind, and she asked, "What would be your reaction if I suggested that Steven Moretti may have committed suicide?"

The no-nonsense woman replied, "I wouldn't believe it."

"Why not?"

"It's true that I didn't know him well and had no idea what went on in his personal or business life, but I knew him well enough to be sure that suicide is out of the question. The man liked himself too much for that."

"That's an interesting observation," Huber said.

Then she declared, "I promised you a short interview and had best end it before you call me a liar." And getting up, she said, "Should you remember the name of the English woman, or if you recall anything out of the ordinary about Mr. Moretti and his household, please call." And she handed over her business card.

As Huber walked to her car, she thought; the housekeeper is sharp, no question about that. And Bart Trimboli is correct in his opinion that it would be hard to tag her with a motive.

CHAPTER 21

The corporate headquarters office of Cucina di Enzo was located on Brand Boulevard in one of the high-rise buildings making up the main downtown skyline of Glendale. On Friday, June 8, shortly after 5 o'clock, the board of directors meeting came to an end.

Marco Valente asked the assembled, "Is there another motion on the table?"

No one spoke up.

"In that case, meeting adjourned."

The secretary who had taken the minutes closed her laptop, and as the board members scrambled to their feet, Marco Valente, the new CEO, held two people back, saying, "Claudia and Kevin, just a moment." And when everyone else had left the conference room, he told them, "There is a Mrs. Huber looking into Steven's murder. She wants to talk to us, one at the time. I thought it best to have her come here after the board meeting, rather than interviewing us during the course of the day in our own offices."

Kevin Gasparian asked, "Why?"

"It's less conspicuous this way. Everyone is hurrying out the door on a Friday."

"I meant, why is the woman asking questions? Is she working for Rachel's attorney?"

"She's a private investigator. I don't know who hired her, but since we have nothing to hide, it's prudent to cooperate. I told her that we can each give her fifteen minutes."

Claudia Chambers said, "I wanted to finish some work in my office. When is she coming?"

Marco checked the time and said, "At 5:15, which is just about now. Go ahead and take care of your task. You can be the last person to get interviewed." Then he addressed them both, "I have no idea what the investigator is after, but under no circumstances give out any information about the company's finances or other sensitive inside data. Those topics are none of her business."

Huber stepped off the elevator on the 12th floor of the high-rise, where Marco Valente welcomed her. If surprised at her age and slight physique, he didn't show it. For her part, Huber did a quick appraisal. The man was in his early thirties, of average height and weight, had short dark hair, brown eyes, and a prominent Adam's apple.

Cucina di Enzo, Incorporated, occupied the entire floor, and he guided her along deserted cubicles to the conference room, saying, "The staff has left for the weekend. Only the two executives you asked to talk with and myself are still on the premises."

Once Huber and the CEO were seated at the elongated conference table, Valente said, "You can start with me."

"I appreciate that," Huber replied. Then she got straight to the point and said, "I've gone to San Diego to see Mr. Enzo Moretti. He enlightened me about the founding of his original restaurant and its progression into a chain enterprise under the leadership of his son. He also shared that you are now taking on the job of CEO. What was your position before Steven Moretti died, by the way?"

"I had the title of COO."

With an apologetic smile, she admitted, "I'm not well versed in corporate titles. What does that stand for?"

"Chief Operating Officer," he replied.

"And you are related to the Moretti family?"

"So he also told you that! I'm a distant relative; Enzo Moretti and my father are second cousins."

"Do you hope to inherit the business when Mr. Moretti, Sr., dies?"

He gave her a perplexed look and replied, "I don't know the content of his will, but that is unlikely."

"Who will be the heir, in your opinion?"

"Steven would have been; he was co-owner to begin with. Now I don't know who'll come into the business after the old gentleman passes on. Your guess is as good as mine. Maybe his other son, Keith, is the lucky devil, even though he left the company."

Huber nodded and said, "Mr. Moretti told me about Keith and that there had been an argument between the brothers."

"He sure told you a lot!"

"What was their conflict?"

Annoyed, he replied, "They had different views on business strategy, and I'm not going to lay it out for you."

"Forgive me, I didn't mean to pry into any company secrets. Still, I'd be interested to know whose side you were on."

"That's a no-brainer," he replied. "Steven was right 99% of the time, and that dispute did not fall into the 1% category."

"I take it that he had a great knack for business."

"He was a genius and it won't be easy for me to fill his shoes."

Huber stated, "I can see that you admired his accomplishments as the company's CEO. What did you think of him as a man?"

"Ditto!"

"You also admired him as a person?"

"You heard me."

"I understand that he had a bit of the Casanova in him."

"What's wrong with that? Women flocked to him like hens around a rooster, so why not take advantage? After all, he was single and not breaking any laws. I wish I had his looks and luck with the ladies."

Huber studied the man's average features, trying hard not to focus on his large Adam's apple bobbing up and down as he talked, and asked, "You are also single?"

He gave an embarrassed chuckle and said, "Actually, I'm married. I made the comment just as a figure of speech."

"Was your relationship with Steven Moretti strictly a business matter, or did you also see him socially?"

"We didn't hang out in bars and clubs together, if that's what you're asking, but we did see each other occasionally outside the firm."

"For example?"

"At Christmas parties, company picnics, employee weddings, that sort of thing. And once in a blue moon my wife and I got invited to a Moretti clan get-together in San Diego."

"Did you go to Steven's engagement party?"

"Yes, and to his housewarming too."

"So you've met Rachel Penrose. What did you think of her?"

"I liked her and thought that she and Steven were compatible, which doesn't make me a good judge of people, I have to admit."

"How about Jasmine Dewitt?"

"Who is that?"

"Jasmine works at Club Marzipan as an exotic dancer."

"Oh, you mean the stripper. I didn't know her name. To answer your question, I've never had the pleasure of meeting her."

He checked his watch and Huber knew her time with him was up.

CHAPTER 22

Kevin Gasparian was middle-aged, had curly hair graying at the temples, and wore glasses. A hint of a minor pot-belly above his belt showed through the white Oxford dress-shirt as he walked into the conference room. That he was a man of few words soon became evident to Huber.

She greeted him with, "Sorry to impose on you on a Friday evening, Mr. Gasparian."

He didn't respond, just nodded his head in acknowledgement and took a chair.

Huber started the interview with, "What is your position at Cucina di Enzo, Incorporated?"

"I'm the CFO," he replied.

"Would that stand for Chief Financial Officer?"

"Correct."

"I'd like to get your opinion of Mr. Steven Moretti."

"He was an excellent CEO."

"Did you enjoy working for him?"

"Yes."

"Was he well liked?"

"I wouldn't know. He got the job done and that's all that counts."

"And what did you think of him on a personal level?"

"I never had a problem with him."

"I heard that he was a bit of a ladies' man, is that right?"

"If you say so."

Huber did not show her frustration. She had interviewed plenty of tongue-tied people in the past and knew that showing annoyance on her part would make him even less willing to talk. She patiently waited a few seconds and then changed her line of questioning.

She asked, "How is Mr. Valente working out as your new CEO?"

"He'll do."

"But?"

"The man is no Steven Moretti."

Finally, Huber thought, I'm getting a bit of a reaction out of him! She said, "Mr. Moretti was top drawer?"

"You got it. He knew all about business and could also handle people."

"Did you see him socially?"

"Rarely."

"I understand that he and Rachel Penrose gave a lavish engagement party. Did you attend?"

Gasparian replied, "I was out of town at the time."

"What about their housewarming? Were you around for that?"

"Yes, we went."

"Did you enjoy yourselves?"

Taken by surprise with that question, he thought about it, and then said, "My wife Marla did, I think."

"But you didn't?"

Again he took his time with answering and then said, "Social gatherings are not my thing."

With the man's profession in mind and how this interview was proceeding, Huber mused, he prefers numbers to people. That's obvious.

Aloud she said, "What do you think of Rachel Penrose?"

"I hardly know her."

"Still, one gets a first impression."

He admitted, "I liked her fine."

"Do you believe her guilty of Steven Moretti's murder?"

"Isn't that a fact?"

Huber replied, "She has not been on trial nor convicted yet." And she inquired, "Have you ever heard of Jasmine Dewitt?"

"No."

Then she gave him an encouraging smile and asked, "What is your opinion of your business associates at Cucina di Enzo, Incorporated? I'm mainly thinking of the board of directors."

"They're all capable people."

"What about their personalities outside the company?"

"I have no interest in their private lives," Kevin Gasparian stated.

CHAPTER 23

A couple of minutes later, Claudia Chambers joined Huber in the conference room. She wore a light-gray pinstripe suit with a bright red blouse and pumps, and kept her caramel-colored hair in a short stylish do. Purpose and determination showed in her strong features. Even her stride was commanding.

She sat down and without giving Huber a chance to ease into the interview, took charge herself and said, "I'm Claudia Chambers, CIO, and may or may not be promoted to COO."

Huber said, "Chief Operating Officer was the position Marco Valente held before Steven Moretti's death. Are you next in line?"

"I would think so, but one never knows; somebody new may get hired."

"What does CIO stand for, by the way?"

"Chief Information Officer. Looks like you've come to the right person," she replied with a smirk. And in the same breath, she continued, "I understand you're seeking information about the late Steven Moretti."

Huber did not mind giving up the driver's seat. On the contrary, letting Ms. Chambers be in command revealed a lot of the woman's disposition. So she just nodded.

The CIO went on, "Steven was a wizard in his field with a natural instinct to turn any deal to his and the company's advantage. He also tended to be a clever manipulator. His genius went way beyond what they taught him at university getting his business major. In short, the man was brilliant!"

"You liked working under him, then?"

"Loved it! He had an invigorating effect on me." And without any prompting from Huber, she said, "I assume you talked to lots of people already, and if they were honest, you learned that Steven was a womanizer."

"Yes, that's what I heard. Is it true?"

"Every man has a vice. With Steven it involved women. He pursued just about every obtainable female within the company and outside of it. He was drop-dead gorgeous and a smooth operator. Naturally, most office staff women were flattered."

"Were you?"

For the first time Ms. Chambers hesitated before she spoke, and then said, "He didn't approach me. I'd like to think that my being a board member caused his lack of attention, but I'd be kidding myself."

Huber kept silent and just looked at the other woman, knowing that more would come.

Sure enough, she continued, "Steven was impressed by and liked to work with take-charge people, but kept what he considered domineering women out of his bedroom." And an involuntary smile escaped her as she added, "In my opinion, he and Rachel Penrose were well suited."

"Actually, I wanted to ask you what you thought of Rachel," Huber managed to inquire.

"I only saw her a few times and don't know her well, but I did like her. And doing what she did *when* she did it, shows that she wasn't a gold digger, or she'd have waited until after they were married."

"That's an interesting point. And there is no doubt in your mind that Rachel is the killer?"

"None!"

"Are you single, Ms. Chambers?"

"I'm divorced. My ex was a wimp and couldn't handle a powerful spouse."

Not giving her a chance to further elaborate on the shortcomings of the ex-husband, Huber changed the subject and asked, "Do you know Keith Moretti?"

"Of course, I've been on the board for many years and saw him often during his time with us."

"What did you think of him?"

"He tried to keep pace with his brother, but never came close. Being a poor business man and lacking Steven's genius brain as well as his charismatic personality, Keith gave up and left the company."

"How is Marco Valente fitting into the position of CEO?"

With surprising vehemence she replied, "I miss Steven and take offense to the way Marco already throws his weight around! He'll never be able to replace him; nobody can."

There followed a long pause, and then Huber said, "I understand that Steven and Rachel gave an engagement party last September. Did you attend?"

"Yes, it was a gala event held on Coronado Island near San Diego. I also went to their open house in January. They lived in a gorgeous place in La Cañada Flintridge. And of course, I planned to be at their wedding reception on the Queen Mary."

Huber said, "I knew that they gave a housewarming party but not that it was an open house."

"Sure, people were coming and going all day."

Then Huber asked, "Does the name Jasmine Dewitt ring a bell?"

"I think that's the exotic dancer. I never heard of her until after Steven got poisoned."

Huber glanced at her watch and then said, "Fifteen minutes, exactly! Have a great weekend, Ms. Chambers, and good luck with your promotion!"

CHAPTER 24

On Monday morning, June 11, Huber sat at the desk in her office, the open Rachel Penrose file in front of her, mulling over her options once more. Although Peter had been physically home all weekend, mentally he was unavailable, going through one of his creative spurts in the writing of his current manuscript. When this happened, Peter kept glued to his laptop, isolating himself from the rest of the world for days, barely showing up for meals. Consequently, Huber had been left to do little else than dwell on her case for the last 48 hours. She finally came to a decision, reached for the phone, and made several calls.

At home, lingering over coffee after dinner that evening, Peter said, "I never asked how your interviews went with the elite of Cucina di Enzo."

"Welcome to the real world, Peter!"

"Was I that bad?"

"Worse, but I'm used to it," she teased, and told him all about her talks with the board of directors.

He paid attention and then said, "Sounds like Steven Moretti was a superb business man."

"I already knew that before, but yes, all three confirmed it."

"And none of them knew him well on a private level?"

"That's what they say."

"You think they may be lying?"

"I'm obviously grasping at straws here; there is no reason to suspect that they're not telling the truth."

Peter scratched his head and said, "Too bad that both men weren't much of a source for information, but at least the woman seemed more generous with her comments."

"Yes, but sometimes *not telling* reveals a lot."

"Huh?"

"For instance, Marco Valente was uncomfortable with my questions about being related to the Morettis and a possible inheritance of the business."

"I can imagine that the subject may be awkward for him should he have hopes in that direction. By the way, why did you ask them if they'd known or heard of the stripper beforehand?"

Regula replied, "I just did a bit of digging, trying to find some kind of a link, but obviously failed."

"Funny how everyone you've talked to seems to like Rachel, yet they're convinced that she is guilty of the murder."

"An arrest, even if the person is not convicted yet, can have that effect on people. We humans are programmed to believe the obvious."

"But you, of course, are sure of her innocence."

"Far from it; I can't cross her off my suspect list."

Then he asked, "What did you make of Claudia Chambers' remarks about why Moretti didn't hit on her?"

"That told volumes. She was miffed."

"You mean she wanted him to?"

"I'm sure of it. And I wouldn't be surprised if *she* approached *him* and got rejected."

Peter said, "That would make a dent in any woman's ego, even more so in someone as self-assured and aggressive as you describe her."

After a pause he asked, "So what's next on your agenda?"

"I still have a few more people on my list to talk to, and I also made a bunch of phone calls today."

"Evidently the calls were important. So out with it!"

"Something has puzzled me all along," she said. "If Rachel added the oleander to the tea on that Thursday when she went to get her stuff, Steven should have died that very day or the next morning, not three days later. Assuming, of course, that he drank tea every day. Since Rachel seemed the obvious person to know this, I called her. She didn't pick up, so I sent a text message and she texted back within a couple of hours with the info that Steven drank his tea every morning and most evenings after dinner. So unless she's lying - - I can't rule that out - - the timing is off."

"What does that mean?"

"I haven't figured it out exactly, but it could mean good news for Rachel. According to the housekeeper, the tea shipments came from England, and Steven himself added more tea to the canister whenever he ran low on tea leaves."

Peter remarked with a chuckle, "Simple. All you have to do is find another culprit who added the poisonous oleander on the day of his death."

"Piece of cake," she replied with sarcasm. "I'll just call on all the suspects again and ask if any of them dropped by Steven Moretti's place and wandered into the backyard on his last day, and surely the villain will admit to it!"

They had switched from dining room to living room, getting ready to watch a movie when Regula commented, "I also called Enzo Moretti to find out when he's expecting

another visit from his son Keith and learned that's not
likely to happen until Christmas. Needless to say that
I can't wait that long to talk with him. Rachel's trial is
scheduled for August."

"Do you know where he is at the moment?"

"According to his father, the man is currently executive
chef on an Alaskan cruise liner."

"So what are you going to do? Is he reachable by
phone, or can you set up a Skype session?"

"There's nothing better than an interview in person,"
she stated. "I've always wanted to take an Alaskan cruise."

"Oh no, Regula! Count me out. I'm not interested in
seeing a bunch of glaciers, even if you argue that they're
fast melting away."

"I know that you hate going on cruises, particularly
to cold Alaska. I wouldn't dream of asking you to come
along."

"Good. As long as that's clear."

His spouse continued, "Andi's spring semester is
almost over. Classes ended last Friday and after finals
this week, she'll be free. I'm thinking of taking her on the
cruise."

The previews were over and the movie was about to
start, so they put any further conversation on hold.

Not until they were ready for bed and turned off the
lights did Peter ask, "Is that client of yours - - what's his
name?"

"Jonathan Lighthart?"

"Right. Is he paying for your and Andi's cruise as well
as the airfare to wherever the ship is taking off from?"

He could not see the grin on her face in the dark when
she replied, "That's another call I made today, and he's
willing to go fifty/fifty."

"One of the things I love about you," Peter teased, "is
how you drive a hard bargain."

CHAPTER 25

On Wednesday afternoon of that week, Tina Brook labored over her stained glass project in the studio of her residence in the upscale neighborhood of La Cañada Flintridge. She was applying putty into the gaps of the stained glass panel, wiping off excess with a rag. As she was in the process of applying putty to the other side, the doorbell rang. Damn it, she thought, that must be the investigator. I shouldn't have gotten involved with this project after coming home from work. Too late now; she'll just have to wait a couple of minutes.

In front of the residence, Huber waited in anticipation of a promising interview with Rachel's friend.

Irritated, Tina pulled off her latex gloves just as Huber pushed the bell a second time, and making her way to the front of the house she hollered, "Coming!" Opening the door, still wearing her protective mask and apron she said, "Come in. I'm in the middle of something," and Huber followed her through the entry, down the hallway, all the way to the back door leading out to the yard. They walked past a lemon tree heavy with fruit and by a row of blooming pink shrubs.

Tina guided Huber to a paved patio, furnished with garden table and chairs, mumbling, "Please wait here."

Then she walked the few steps to the small studio structure, opened the wide sliding-glass door, went inside and slid the door closed firmly behind her. Huber sensed Tina was bothered by the interruption, but instead of sitting down in the patio area, she stationed herself at the glass door looking in at the artist's work place.

There was an elongated work bench in the center of the room where Tina was putting on a fresh pair of protective gloves and began sprinkling polishing powder on her work to clean it up, scrubbing with a dry bristle brush. Then Huber watched as she carefully flipped the panel over and repeated the process on the other side. It seemed extremely messy, with particles and dust flying all about. No wonder the woman protected herself with a mask, Huber thought. With the job finished, Tina fetched a vacuum cleaner from the closet and thoroughly vacuumed the entire room. Only then did she take off the mask, latex gloves, and apron before opening the sliding-glass door.

She said, "Sorry, that was bad timing, but I couldn't take the chance to interrupt the procedure and let the putty dry as it would be difficult to remove later on. Let's go in the house." And with a sudden grin she asked, "You *are* Mrs. Huber, right?"

"Yes, that's me, and I'm happy to meet you, Mrs. Brook. You got me interested, though. I see that you're savvy in the art of stained glass. May I have a peek at your studio?"

"Be my guest," the tall young woman said, ushering her into the room, "and please call me Tina."

With the mask removed, Huber briefly studied Tina's face. She had a healthy, natural look about her with intelligent light-brown eyes, shoulder-length dark hair parted on the side, a generous mouth, and a few freckles spread over her nose.

Huber admired the finished stained glass art displayed throughout the room. There were several free-hanging stained contemporary glass panels with geometric designs. An exquisite window hanging dangling in a solid oak frame in particular caught Huber's eye. The colored transparent glass and clear pre-cut beveled glass was a creation of four large tulip shapes and beveled squares that were arranged to let the sun shine through, flooding the area with prism rainbows.

Huber swept her arm in an all-encompassing gesture and asked, "You created all these?"

"Sure," Tina replied, "and many more."

"They are beautiful! Is this a hobby, or are you in the stained glass business?"

"It started out as a hobby. I made several pieces for our own enjoyment and gave some to relatives and close friends as presents. Somehow, word got around and people started to place orders. I'm selective with work I will accept and only agree to do pieces I really enjoy making, and I never consent to any kind of deadline. The art of stained glass is therapeutic for me, and I don't want it to become stressful."

Huber gazed at the stained glass piece on the workbench which Tina had been laboring over and said, "I love stained glass art and often wondered how it is made. Are you willing to share a few tricks of the trade?"

"No problem," she said. "I am using the ancient technique of working with flat stained glass as used in early churches and still being done by glass studios and artists today.

"You start with a design which will be enlarged to the desired finished size. Draw a small grid over the design and transfer it to a proportionately larger grid the size of the final glass project. Then you work in layers: the cartoon on top, carbon paper next, with heavy pattern paper on the bottom. Trace the shapes on the cartoon with a ballpoint pen so the lines will transfer to the pattern paper on the bottom, numbering each one as you go. Cut the pattern paper pieces. Either glue or tape each pattern piece on top of the appropriate glass, then run the glass cutter around the edges.

"Then you place all the pieces on the cartoon, making sure they are a perfect fit. Start the leading process by first stretching the lead came in a vise. Cut the pieces as needed to fit around the glass shapes, hammering in horseshoe nails in order to hold everything tightly in place. Then you flux and solder the joints with the electric soldering iron. When one side is completed, carefully flip the panel over and repeat the process on the reverse side, followed by applying window putty to both sides of the panel. You must do the next step immediately or the putty will dry."

She grinned and stated, "At this point in my work you showed up! As you could see, the job is messy and dangerous. One must wear a face mask to prevent inhaling lead particles and fumes, as well as a heavy apron and latex gloves. Now I'm letting the entire piece set up for at least 24 hours before I finish it with a good quality spray window cleaner."

Huber said, "Amazing how the same work process has been applied for centuries. Thank you for a great lesson," and glancing once more around the room she pointed to the tulip shapes window hanging and remarked, "This one is magnificent!"

Tina's face suddenly changed to a glum expression as she stated, "It was going to be a wedding present for Rachel. Tulips are her favorite flowers."

CHAPTER 26

Tina and Huber walked back into the house and sat down on the comfortable upholstered club chairs in the den where the actual interview began.

Huber asked, "So you're an artist by profession?"

"Wrong. I do indulge in my stained glass arts projects, but I'm an elementary school teacher."

"A fine job requiring patience and dedication."

"I enjoy the work. My husband and I don't have any children, so the students are my substitute kids."

Huber said, "Now let's get to the purpose I came to see you."

Tina blurted, "I'm so glad Rachel hired you to find the real guilty person. She's been so out of it lately that I fear she'll go to her slaughter like a lamb."

Huber asked, "So you believe she's innocent of the murder?"

"I know she's in big doo-doo, but I don't think for a moment that she killed Steven. There has to be another explanation."

"Any suggestion?"

"Not off hand, but I'm sure Steven made enemies. I understand that he ran his business in a cut-throat manner. Or maybe his playing the field finally backfired. I can imagine that he left a few revengeful husbands or boyfriends in his wake."

"So you knew of his infidelities to Rachel?"

"I didn't know it as a fact. Early on in their relationship I had my suspicions. He had macho good looks and a way with women. His wit and charm wasn't lost even on me." She winked and added, "Had to be careful as not to make my husband jealous. But seriously, as time went on, I came to realize how devoted and in love Steven was with Rachel. They were a perfect match."

Huber said, "It's encouraging to learn that you believe in Rachel's innocence. I've interviewed many people concerned in her case, and the majority think that she is guilty."

Tina shrugged and said, "They're wrong."

"How did you meet the pair?"

"I've known Rachel for ages and consider her my best friend. We tell each other our deepest, darkest secrets. Not that Rachel ever has much to confess; she's an angel. As for Steven, my husband and I met him on a skiing and boarding trip to Mammoth, arranged by our ski club. Actually, Rachel met him on the same trip. I felt so happy that she had finally found someone to keep up with her. Rachel is an expert skier and the runs she likes to take are too challenging for the rest of us. I'm an intermediate snowboarder and stay away from black diamond runs. Right away, Steven and Rachel were drawn to each other like a magnet, and not only because of the skiing."

"May I ask how long you've been married?"

"Shane and I tied the knot five years ago."

"And you sure have a lovely home. What a coincidence that Steven and Rachel also moved to La Cañada Flintridge."

"That's not a coincidence. When Steven looked into buying a home, I pointed out having seen one on the market a few houses down the street from us. It turned out that Rachel fell in love with it and he put in a bid."

"So you actually lived on the same street?"

"Yeah, it was great having my friend so close. I'd have been her maid of honor at their wedding they'd planned on the Queen Mary." She sighed and continued, "Now the house is on the market again and I cringe every time I drive by it."

"Oh, I think I saw the 'for sale' sign on my way over. Is it the second property on the left when turning into your street?"

"That's the one."

Then Huber said, "I understand that Steven and Rachel gave a housewarming party. Describe the event to me, please."

"They had an open house. Shane and I stayed for a good part of it. Caterers provided the food; lots of appetizers, but also lunch with a nice selection of hot dishes. People stood around and mingled, the way it's customary at a cocktail party. We were introduced to folks we hadn't met before and likewise chatted with others whom we already knew. At one point, Rachel gave a tour of the house and garden. I had seen it all before, but Shane hadn't, so I tagged along. Rachel, clever in the role of tour guide and hostess, cracked little jokes as she guided people through the rooms and backyard."

Huber asked, "What was there to see in the yard?"

"Lots of things; although they kept the pool covered in January, some people sat around it in lounge chairs on that relatively mild day. Rachel proudly showed off her herb garden. She grew not just your average parsley and chives plants, but a first-rate gourmet herbs and spice nursery with thyme, oregano, rosemary, basil, tarragon, peppermint, and dill. She also nurtured a sage shrub and a wasabi root. Her most cherished and expensive spice was saffron, which she extracted from the saffron crocus flower."

She paused and then continued, "Located at the very end of the yard stood the cursed oleander bush. And don't be influenced by what Rachel said about it; that was just an unfortunate remark."

"What remark?" Huber asked.

Surprised, Tina said, "I assumed that someone told you about it. In hindsight it sounds eerie, but Rachel made a silly comment while taking people on the tour of the yard. Walking near the oleander bush she said, 'This plant is extremely poisonous,' and pointing at Steven who was entertaining some women sitting by the pool, joked, 'He'd better behave or I'll put some of its leaves in his tea!'"

"Interesting."

"She didn't mean anything by it - - everyone laughed - - but of course the stupid little joke she made then sounds incriminating now."

"Interesting, for sure," Huber repeated. And she inquired, "Do you recall who was close enough to overhear the remark?"

"That would include lots of people. Let me think - - there were two men and a woman from Steven's work, all board of directors; his father and brother; an old friend by the name of Bart. Then there was Zack Jefferson - - Steven's would-be best man - - with wife and adorable little kids. Oh, I almost forgot, Jonathan, who is Rachel's friend, tagged along, and of course Shane and I were part of the group."

"That's roughly ten people who made up Rachel's garden tour and heard her comment, or do you remember anyone else?"

"Rachel's friends, mostly women, were sitting by the pool area where Steven had stopped to talk, but I'm sure they were too far away to hear."

"Now let's move on to the events at the beginning of April. When did you learn that Rachel walked in on her cheating fiancé?"

"Right away; she called me on the same evening. She'd freaked out and couldn't think clearly. I offered to contact everyone to call the wedding off, if that's what she wanted. After all, it was only ten days away. I already had the wedding party people's info, and Rachel e-mailed me the long guest list. I asked her if she also wanted me to get in touch with the coordinator or the Queen Mary staff, but she said she had better do that herself or let Steven deal with the unpleasant task, as most of the wedding had been pre-paid."

At that moment they heard the front door being opened and then footsteps sounding down the hall before Shane Brook joined them in the den.

He shook Huber's hand and then went over to kiss his wife, asking "Am I interrupting?"

Huber said, "Not at all. I hope that you've got time to join us in the conversation."

He took off his coat and tie and said, "Tina told me all about you and what you're trying to discover. My workday is over, so my time is all yours "

"May I ask what you do for a living?"

"I work at a bank."

Tina put in, "Don't be modest, Shane." And to Huber, "He is vice president of Premium Western Bank in Pasadena."

He looked embarrassed and said, "Let's not talk about me. I'd like to help with your investigation but don't have a clue as to who might be the real killer. I've given it a lot of thought but came away empty."

"Am I correct in presuming that you've lost a good friend in Steven Moretti?"

"True. Tina and Rachel have been friends for many years, and ever since Steven came into Rachel's life, the four of us socialized as we had lots in common. Steven was highly entertaining; we've shared good times together."

Huber asked, "How did you first learn of the tragic event that happened on April 8? Did someone let you know or did you read about it in the paper?"

Shane answered, "We were on our way to go out to dinner on that Sunday night and saw the ambulance parked in Steven's driveway. I stopped and we got out of the car just as the paramedics wheeled him from the house. They didn't give us any information, just told us to step out of the way."

He cleared his throat and continued, "We went ahead with our plans of dining out, but had lost our appetites. Steven was nonstop on our minds. Later, Tina called the hospital trying to find out what happened and was eager to get news about his condition."

Tina took over and said, "They told me nothing since it is against hospital policy to give non-family members information about the status of a patient. Not until I phoned his dad on Monday did I learn of Steven's death. Then it occurred to me that Rachel probably didn't know, so I called and broke the news to her."

Huber addressed them both, inquiring, "When did you last see Steven Moretti alive?"

Husband and wife looked at each other, trying to recall the exact day. Then Shane said, "Must have been when we flew up to North Shore Lake Tahoe for a ski weekend at the beginning of March."

"That's right," Tina agreed. "No, wait, I briefly saw him once more on the following weekend when I gave

Rachel a wedding shower. He came here after it was over and walked her home."

"Have you seen Rachel in the last two months?"

Shane replied, "I saw her once and she is different."

"That's an understatement," Tina said. "I've seen her three times and had to push myself on her, at that. She is a shadow of her former self. Please find the real murderer so that she can have a life again."

"I'm giving it my best effort."

Huber got up to leave and, turning to Tina, said, "You mentioned a would-be best man. I don't have him on my contact list. What is his name again, and do you know where he lives?"

"That's Zack Jefferson. He works in Simi Valley as a software developer. I forgot where he lives. Hold on, I'll get his number."

She was back in a flash with Zack's phone number scribbled on a piece of paper, and handing it over said, "He lives all the way out in Camarillo, but I didn't write down his address."

"His number is all I need, thank you."

Minutes later, Huber drove by Steven Moretti's former residence. She slowed down and read a notice propped up next to the "for sale" sign. It read, "Open House, Saturday June 16." I'll keep it in mind, she told herself.

CHAPTER 27

The next day, Huber searched the web for a last-minute deal on the Alaskan cruise liner where Keith Moretti was employed. The ship sailed from Vancouver, Canada on Wednesday, June 20. That gives us six days before departure; definitely doable, she thought. She compared flight schedules to Vancouver for Tuesday or Wednesday morning on several airline sites when interrupted by a phone call from Rufina Ramos.

"Oh, Mrs. Ramos, you remembered the English woman's name?"

The housekeeper replied, "No, but you said I should let you know if I remember anything else. It probably means nothing, but the other day something about the last tea shipment popped into my head."

Huber had quickly pulled the Rachel Penrose file when hearing Mrs. Ramos's voice, and leafing through it now said, "You mean the shipment from Tea Brewer that arrived on Thursday, March 29?"

"That's right. The Tea Brewer label on the package looked the same as always, but this parcel came from within the United States. Before that, all tea shipments were mailed from England. So I assumed that the company had found a distributor in the US."

"That's interesting. So you noticed the US postmark. What town was the package sent from?"

"I have no idea. I didn't look at the postmark, but it had no customs declaration form attached. When the mailman handed the package over, I asked about the form, and he said the shipment came from the US. Like I said, it probably means nothing, but you told me to call if I remembered anything unusual."

"And you say that the shipping label had the Tea Brewer logo that they normally sent from England?"

"Yes, I'm sure. It had a unique picture of a tea kettle on the top left corner."

"You didn't perchance open the package and keep the box with the label?"

The housekeeper was offended and said, "Definitely not! I'd never open any package or mail that isn't addressed to me."

"Oh, I wouldn't suggest any such thing. I thought it possible that Mr. Moretti had instructed you to open tea shipments for him."

"No, he didn't. I put the package unopened on the kitchen counter since I knew it contained his loose leaf tea."

Huber stated, "This bit of news may be important to my investigation. I'll give it some thought. Thank you for letting me know."

In the evening, Huber called Andi, whom she had not talked to since their fondue night. She clued her in on her visit to corporate headquarters of Cucina di Enzo, the interviews with Tina and Shane Brook, as well as the one with Rufina Ramos, including the housekeeper's call of that day.

Andi heard her out and then commented, "So the Cucina di Enzo business has an entire floor at a high-rise on Brand Boulevard in Glendale. Sounds like a snazzy outfit."

"Believe me, it is!"

Huber heard the mockery in Andi's voice as she said, "But that Claudia woman is not above chatting you up with some gossip!" Then she remarked, "I kinda like the Brook couple. Are they as nice as you make them out?"

Huber said, "Yes, they are, and good friends of both Rachel and the late Steven. But then, some of the seemingly nicest people turn out to be murderers."

"Rufina is a smart cookie for sure. What's your take on the tea package not being mailed from England? You think it was tampered with?"

"That's a possibility. I need to reflect on the matter in detail. And now to another subject: When is your last final?"

"Tomorrow."

"That's what I thought. How about joining me on an Alaskan cruise?"

"You're jivin', boss!"

"I'm dead serious."

"Holy Krewe! You're invitin' me to go on a cruise! I've never been on an ocean cruise or to Alaska. I'm tickled pink!"

Huber smiled to herself. Whenever Andi got either excited or angry, her Southern drawl became acute. She was clearly excited at that moment.

Andi slowed down some and said, "I reckon we're takin' the voyage to tackle Steven's brother."

"Correct. But enjoying the adventure while we're at it is allowed."

"When are we leaving?"

"Tuesday of next week. Can you be ready?"

"I'll start packing right away!"

"We are flying to Vancouver, Canada, where we board the ship on the next day. Do you have a valid passport?"

"Yes, ma'am. You told me a while back to have one made so I'd be ready for anything."

CHAPTER 28

On Saturday R. A. Huber parked on the street near Steven Moretti's former residence and then walked up the wide driveway leading to the front entrance. Two cars were stationed on it, one belonging to the real estate agent, the other to a couple interested in the property. There would have been plenty of space for Huber's vehicle as well, but she preferred approaching on foot to get a feel for the two-level Mediterranean with a close view of the Angeles Forest Mountains.

To get familiarized with basic information, she had looked up the listing that morning which read: "4,200 square feet, 4 bedrooms, 3 ½ baths, formal dining room off the kitchen, spacious living room, family room, 2 fireplaces, 3-car garage, pool and garden. Asking price: $1.45 million." She stepped through the open front door, thinking, I have no idea what I'm looking for in this place, but maybe I'll get a lucky break.

The real estate lady placed her cup of coffee onto the card table set up in the impressive high-ceiling foyer and, rising from her folding chair when Huber entered, announced, "Welcome to our Open House. Feel free to browse and let me know if you have any questions."

"Thank you, I will," Huber replied, passed by her, and then mounted the spiral staircase leading to the second level. The interested couple came out of a bedroom as Huber climbed the last step, and the woman said, "The master suite is exquisite. Your eyes are in for a treat!"

The first thing Huber noticed about the master bedroom was its huge size and that it lacked furniture. She checked out the black marble fireplace, walk-in closet, double-pane windows and French doors going out to a balcony overlooking the pool area. Then she walked over to the adjacent master bathroom and observed that it looked indeed elegant. The double sinks, toilet, and jumbo Jacuzzi bathtub that one walked down two steps into, were all done in black-and-white marble, while the glass-encased shower stood separate. I'd love to bask in this tub, Huber thought. Then she briefly viewed the other three empty bedrooms and baths, as well as a laundry room equipped with washer and dryer, before returning downstairs.

Heading to the kitchen and dining room, she overheard a conversation between the interested party and the real estate agent. The man said, "We like the layout of this house, but it's hard to get a live-in picture in a totally empty home. Has the property been on the market for a long time since the people already moved out?"

"Not at all," the agent replied. "It has only been listed for two weeks as the owner had to relocate."

That's one way of putting it, Huber thought, and couldn't help but smirk.

The kitchen was artfully done in light colors, giving the vast room a cheerful, airy quality. The off-white cabinets above marble top counters made a pleasant contrast to the stainless steel appliances and double sinks. A U-shaped island with an additional prep sink and under-the-counter microwave stood in the center of the room.

Huber continued on her tour through the formal dining room - - which didn't look all that formal with the furniture missing - - the downstairs half bathroom near the foyer, the family room, and ended up in the outsized living room. She found that entire space also bare - - except for the fireplace and light fixtures - - and walked over to the panoramic glass folding doors opening to the patio, pool, and garden. She stepped outside.

There was a built-in barbecue, patio table and chairs, closed sun-umbrella stands, and some lounge chairs scattered around the pool area. Did they forget to pack up the outdoor furniture? Huber mused. She strolled over to the well-kept garden beds of perennials in a spectacular burst of color: white daisies, yellow daylilies, multiple shades of chrysanthemums, bright red poppies, and pink peonies. Near the concrete fence of the property there stretched a bed about 2 ½ x 1 yard of nothing but plain earth. This must be where Rachel kept her herb garden, she deduced.

Then she made her way clear over to the other end of the yard, where she suddenly faced the oleander bush up close. She stared at it for a long time. The thing stood over two yards high, had dark-green spear-shaped leaves, and was in full bloom with beautiful fragrant pink to red flowers growing in clusters at the end of each branch. The plant looked harmless but was obviously lethal. Now, where have I recently seen a whole row of these bushes? she asked herself.

CHAPTER 29

On Monday, June 18, at 5:00 p.m., Huber sat in a Starbuck's in Simi Valley waiting for Zack Jefferson. She was all packed and ready for her trip on the next day. Mr. Jefferson had agreed to meet her at the end of his workday before driving home to his family in Camarillo. Already on the phone he sounded like a man with a sense of humor. He mentioned being African American, but just in case she'd have trouble spotting him in a crowd, he said he'd be wearing a yellow shirt with the engraved logo of his company. She had returned the banter by telling him that he should be on the lookout for a chic old lady dressed in red.

Allowing for traffic jams, Huber arrived 15 minutes early, so she got her espresso, found a table for two, and relaxed. A fair crowd of people gathered in the place, winding down after a day's work. She was amused by two animated young women in close vicinity debating at length whether to wear boots, shoes, or sandals to an event when a man suddenly placed his beverage on her table and sat down on the chair next to her.

Huber turned her head to come face to face with Zack Jefferson in his yellow shirt, hair cropped close to the scalp, enormous glasses perched on the bridge of his nose, and an impish smile on his lips.

She said, "I appreciate your taking the time to talk with me before heading home. You are a software developer, correct?"

"Yeah, not your stereotypical black guy," he replied.

"I'm at a loss what you're referring to."

With a broad grin he announced, "I'm a total nerd and proud of it."

"I'll know whom to call next time I run into computer problems," she joked back.

Then she got down to business and said, "Let's talk about Steven Moretti. I understand that you were going to be his best man, so you must have been good friends. Where did you know him from?"

"We joined the same university fraternity. Steven got himself elected as its president, and I held the job of treasurer."

"So you stayed in close contact for the last ten years or so, right?"

"Wrong. We got into a major fight at the beginning of our senior year. He really pissed me off. I stayed clear of him for the rest of our college life."

Zack did not elaborate and Huber just looked at him, waiting.

After a long silence he blurted "The son of a bitch stole my girlfriend. You don't mess with Zack Jefferson's woman and stay friends."

That last sentence had been uttered with sudden vehemence, making Huber pause for several seconds before she asked, "So how come he ended up choosing you as his best man?"

As quickly as his anger had flared up, it vanished, and he answered in good humor, "About three years ago we ran into each other at the Convention Center, of all places, during the annual L. A. Auto Show. He seemed genuinely pleased to see me, having forgotten all about what a jerk he'd been in college. I let it go also; by that time I was happily married with two kids. We've stayed in touch since then. Cleo - - that's my wife - - and Rachel hit it off, so we hung together often."

"In other words, you'd forgiven him."

"Let's just say I'd let it rest."

"Pertaining to those last three years, what pops into your mind when thinking of Steven Moretti?"

Without hesitation he said, "That'd be 'success'."

"In business?"

"Of course in business, that's obvious. The man knew how to keep an upper hand. Anything he touched turned up roses. In the current economy when many restaurants are folding, his chain enterprise is still prospering. But that's not all I meant. His private life was also a success story. Steven was a great athlete, tended to be the life of any party, and women dug him."

"Now tell me about the recent past. Am I correct in assuming that you and your family were at Steven and Rachel's engagement party as well as their housewarming in January?"

"Sure, but the engagement was a formal affair on Coronado Island where Cleo and I spent the night, so we left the kids with grandma."

"What do you remember about the open house?"

"An upscale two-story home with lots of rooms, an impressive yard and garden around a good-sized pool."

"I've seen the house and that's not what I wanted to know. I hoped you'd tell me about the people."

"There were lots of folks there; some we already knew and others we met for the first time. We didn't know

Steven's father before and chatted with him at length. The old man was nice and our kids took to him right away."

"I'm aware that Rachel took you and several other people on a tour of the property."

"Yeah, she did."

"Do you recall any comment she made?"

"She made lots of 'em as she marched us around the place. Most were witty."

"I'm thinking specifically of something she said when stopping by the oleander bush."

"Oh that!"

"So you do remember her remark?"

"I'd have forgotten all about it if not for my five-year-old son who brought it up when we got home. I explained to him that she'd just been kidding."

He took a long sip of his double latte and then said, "In retrospect, Rachel's words give me the creeps, but at the time I felt positive she meant it as a joke."

"Do you still think so now?"

"As I said, she must have been kidding when saying she'd put oleander leaves in Steven's tea if he didn't behave, but maybe in her subconscious mind - - oh crap, I don't know what to think of it now," he said, exasperated.

"Do you believe that Rachel is guilty of killing Steven?"

"I was shocked when we first heard about the murder, but it sure looks like she's responsible for the crime." And he added, "If you can find another culprit you'd make Cleo real happy. She is convinced of Rachel's innocence, not because she has any facts to back it up, but because she wants her friend to be exonerated."

"I'm giving it my best effort," Huber assured him.

Then she asked, "By the way, how did you first learn of the poisoning?"

Rachel's friend - - can't remember her name right now - - who was to be her maid of honor, called and - -"

"Tina Brook?"

"Yeah, her. She called the wedding off a few days earlier and of course had to give us the reason. Then she got in touch with us again later and broke the bad news about Steven."

"When did you see Steven Moretti last?"

"That'd be April 1, when a bunch of us former fraternity guys gave him a bachelor party."

Huber reached into her purse and pulled out her essential pocket calendar. She checked the date and stated, "April 1 was on Sunday, exactly one week before Mr. Moretti died."

"Right."

"What was it like?"

"Say what?"

The lady detective pointed out, "I've obviously never been to a bachelor party. Describe it to me, please."

He grinned and said, "The usual nonsense: lots of drinking, dirty jokes, gag gifts, and strippers."

"Did Jasmine Dewitt perform?"

"Yes, and she brought along two other dancers from Club Marzipan."

"Did you know Jasmine beforehand?"

"No, she introduced herself and the other strippers when jumping out of a cake. I had no idea that she and Steven were friends. They played it cool that night."

"Who hired the Club Marzipan performers for the bachelor party?"

"One of the fraternity brothers, no doubt, but I don't know who organized the party. In fact, I wasn't all that enthused about showing up for it and only decided at the last minute to go."

"How come?"

"I'm a nerd and don't dig bachelor parties."

"What changed your mind?"

"Cleo did. She thought that Steven's best man shouldn't miss his bachelor party."

"I think I'd like your wife!" Huber remarked.

"Me too," Zack replied with a mischievous grin.

CHAPTER 30

To play fair, Huber called David Wachterman before leaving for the airport and filled him in on some of her findings so far. After all, she had promised to report.

When she got him on the line, he immediately asked, "So you've got a lead for me?"

"Not really a lead, but I'd like to share some facts I've hit upon. First off, I've interviewed two people that were not on your witness list," and she gave details of her talk with Bart Trimboli and Zack Jefferson, including their respective phone numbers.

Wachterman said, "Thank you! That's good to know."

Huber continued, "It dawned on me that the timing is off if, as alleged, Rachel added the oleander to the tea on Thursday, April 5. Steven apparently drank tea every day, so that scenario doesn't make sense."

Wachterman stated, "I'm looking at the file right now, and in that case he should have died on the same day, or possibly the next, not three days later on April 8!"

"Exactly."

"That's a logical conclusion, Mrs. Huber. I should have spotted it myself."

She went on to tell what she had learned from the housekeeper about the last tea shipment not having been sent from England and remarked, "I haven't figured that one out yet, but it's suggestive."

He said, "She didn't let me know about the tea package having been mailed from the US."

"Oh, she only remembered it a few days ago."

Huber kept her trump card for last, mentioning the remark Rachel made when giving the tour of the yard at the housewarming.

The lawyer said, "So she actually joked about poisoning her fiancé with oleander ahead of time while loads of people overheard the comment. I can certainly spin that in our favor."

Huber replied, "I don't care about any spin, Mr. Wachterman. I just want to arrive at the truth."

"Yes, of course."

"That is all I have to report."

"Good work!"

"By the way, I'll be out of reach for eight days, starting now."

"Oh?"

"I'm embarking on a cruise in order to interview Steven Moretti's brother, who works on the ship."

"I must say, you're taking this investigation to great lengths."

"Not at all. I've always longed to have a good excuse for taking a cruise to Alaska!"

Huber heard a hearty laugh coming from the other end of the line, and they ended the call.

CHAPTER 31

They had suffered through airport security at LAX, endured the scrutiny involved with air-travel in the 21st century, had boarded the plane and taken off, and were now twenty minutes into their flight to Vancouver. The seat belt sign was no longer lit, and flight attendants came around taking beverage orders.

Huber put her seat into the reclining position and thought back to the night before when Andi had called, asking if she should pack her piece in the check-in bag, her piece being a Derringer pistol. Huber had stressed that in order to comply with the tough Canadian firearm laws, they'd best leave their guns at home. Even owning permits did not guarantee against having them confiscated either at the airport or when embarking on ship. Besides, there would be no need for any weapons as the purpose of their trip was to have a friendly talk with the victim's brother.

Huber couldn't repress a smile when she recalled the rest of their conversation. She had said, "Since we're on the subject of what to bring, did you pack at least one dress?" Andi had replied, "No, do I need to?" Huber explained that there were bound to be a couple of formal dinners on board ship with the possibility of the captain showing his face. As was typical of Andi, she hadn't given a thought to wardrobe.

When the landscape below faded and the plane soared above the clouds, Andi looked away from the window and, glancing at her boss, caught the smirk on Huber's lips.

Andi asked, "Are we having fun yet?"

"You bet!" Huber responded.

"What are we all doin' on the cruise?"

"I expect that there'll be tons of fun stuff to do on board ship, and I booked us some land excursions: Best of Juneau, Best of Skagway, and Best of Ketchikan. But let's talk shop."

"Yes, ma'am. I've been wondering, is it a done deal that somebody added the oleander to the tea and it couldn't have gotten into Moretti's system in another way, like if he'd inhaled it or somethin'?"

"He definitely swallowed it together with the tea. The authorities found oleander leaves in the canister mixed in with the loose tea leaves, and they also discovered oleander residue among the used tea left in the trash. Why do you ask?"

"I reckon there'd be a weird or nasty taste, so how come he drank it?"

"That occurred to me, but I learned that he added honey to his brew. I assume that the sweetness of the honey would disguise any odd taste."

Then she said, "Let me fill you in on my interview with Zack Jefferson," and she related the talk she'd had with him in Simi Valley.

Andi listened carefully and then asked, "So he wasn't holdin' a grudge anymore?"

"Apparently not."

"He even agreed to be the guy's best man! Did you believe him about no longer being pissed off at Moretti?"

"He seemed sincere, but one never knows."

Andi looked out the window again, staring into the clouds. Seconds passed before she focused her eyes back on Huber and said, "So boss, how do you figure someone other than Rachel had access to the oleander bush in the yard and managed to stay in Moretti's kitchen by him or herself long enough to tamper with the tea in the canister?"

"I can't think of anybody, and that includes Rachel."

"What?"

"If the killer were to have taken the oleander leaves from that bush and dumped them into the tea canister, he would have had to do so on April 8, the day Steven died, or we can stretch that to the day before. April 5 was the last time Rachel stepped on his property, at least that seems common knowledge."

"So what are you saying?"

Huber stated, "I've come to the conclusion that someone could have added oleander to the tea package before mailing it to Steven Moretti."

"Holy Krewe! You think the shipment was snatched. But wait a minute; didn't the housekeeper say it came with a legit label of the English company?"

"Correct."

"I don't get it! Even if the murderer knew when the package was shipped from England, how could he intercept it?"

"I've given this some thought, and it is rather simple. The villain ordered the tea from England, opened the package and added the poisonous oleander leaves, then carefully resealed it. Next, he typed and printed out a plain label addressing it to Steven and affixed it over the Tea Brewer label, making sure not to cover their logo."

Andi asked, "How did he know what company Steven ordered his tea from?"

"My guess is that it came up in conversation between Steven and our culprit. Or what is even more likely is that he mentioned it to a group of people, say, at his engagement party or the housewarming. For instance, the subject of tea versus coffee might have come up and he may have said something like, 'I only drink loose leaf tea now and order it directly from Tea Brewer in England.' And he may have also mentioned the exact blend he preferred."

"That makes sense, but where did the killer get a hold of oleander?"

"The plant is not all that rare; I've seen it recently, but can't for the life of me remember where."

There was severe turbulence making them hold on to their beverage glasses. When the shaking stopped, Andi said, "You think that someone who went to the housewarming and heard Rachel's remark about poisoning Steven got the idea right then and there to frame her?"

"Rachel's comment may have given the person the idea to poison him in that fashion. Whether the person meant to frame her is another matter. Don't forget, at the time Rachel had no motive to kill her fiancé."

"So that pretty much includes all the people you've interviewed."

"Yes, I know, that's a lot of suspects."

Andi deduced, "So even if Rachel is actin' guilty, we can cross her off the list now."

"Not just yet. If indeed the oleander had been mixed in with the tea shipment that arrived at the Moretti household on March 29, then Rachel had no motive for murder at the time it was mailed. Granted, that is just my theory; we don't know it for a fact and cannot rule her out as a suspect."

"Who else had a motive?"

The announcement over the intercom sounded, "This is your flight captain. Please return to your seats, put them in an upright position, and fasten your seat belts. Also refrain from using any electronic devices. We are about to land in Vancouver."

Huber said, "We're going to pick up the question of motives at our next pow-wow."

CHAPTER 32

The taxi driver dropped them off at their hotel in downtown Vancouver. They dined in the hotel restaurant and then went for a brisk neighborhood walk along Granville Street. It was still light outdoors at around nine in the evening, an indication that they were in the vicinity of Northern summer lights.

The next day, going through customs and boarding the ship was organized like Swiss clockwork. The smooth, efficient embarking process of some 2000 passengers was truly a work of organization. Each guest was handed a personal card - the size of a credit card - with a barcode on its backside. The data on these cards had been gathered and processed from each cruise traveler's lengthy check-in form he had previously filled out online. The card had the passenger's name printed on the front and also a large number. Both Huber and Andi's number was 14. This ship card was to be their "good for all" during the next seven days. It served as key to their stateroom, credit card, as well as I.D. while on board, and needed to be shown and scanned when leaving and re-entering the ship at ports.

Their stateroom was located aft on deck 7. It was relatively spacious, sporting a balcony. When they first entered, their luggage had not been delivered yet, so they went for an exploratory tour of the ship. What there was to do and see on this vessel could have kept anyone busy for a month!

Upon returning to their cabin, their luggage was brought, and they had barely unpacked and settled in when the ship started to move. They hurried out onto their balcony, waving to bystanders at the pier as their "home" for the next week glided out of Vancouver harbor.

A short while later, the captain made the announcement on the ship's loudspeaker, "All passengers are asked to assemble on the promenade deck near their assigned lifeboats for an emergency drill." It became clear that the two women's designated lifeboat was number 14.

Andi said, "Oh, I get it; that's the number on our cards."

After finding their way to the promenade deck, they assembled among a group of fellow lifeboat number 14 people. Soon a ship's officer showed the group how to don a lifejacket and gave instructions on what to do in an emergency should leaving the ship become mandatory. It was all rather boring but definitely important to know.

CHAPTER 33

On Thursday, June 21, they woke up to overcast skies and rain, so there wasn't much to see on their scenic cruising of the Inside Passage. They spent the day taking advantage of the fun and informative things to do on board ship. There were shops, a salon and spa, a fitness center, a fine art gallery, a photo gallery, internet access at the Explorations Café, a digital workshop room, several restaurants and bars that included a 24-hour buffet, showrooms, and of course the Casino, to name a few. The countless activities to choose from ranged from pursuits like indoor cycling, golf chipping challenge, pathway to Pilates, and learning to line dance, to less physical endeavors such as a kitchen tour, creative crafts class, team trivia, the art of flower arranging, et cetera.

Huber joined a group of fellow passengers in the cosmic Wii bowling challenge and managed to become a finalist, only to be eliminated in the next frame. Later she attended a class in the digital workshop to learn how to operate her brand-new camera she had purchased especially for the trip. There had been no time to print out the countless user's manual pages, let alone study them before the voyage.

Andi opted to go for a swim and then hung around the pool, where she got challenged to a Ping-Pong match.

In the late afternoon, they met up in their stateroom and Huber said, "We need to set up an appointment with Keith Moretti."

"Sure thing, boss," Andi remarked. "How are we goin' to do that? Think we have to go through the captain?"

"Let's hope that there is an easier way."

A few minutes later, they were in line at the front office on the main deck. Once at the counter, they showed their magic ship cards and Huber said, "We are private investigators and would like to make arrangements to have an interview with the executive chef."

"Is there a problem?" the employee asked.

"Not at all. We just need to ask Keith Moretti some questions unrelated to your ship. About 20 minutes of his time would be greatly appreciated."

"I'll see what I can do. Check with me again after dinner," the young man behind the desk replied.

That evening happened to be the first formal dinner. Most people dressed accordingly, and Huber was proud to see Andi looking stunning in a simple little black dress. Needless to say, the four-course dinner tasted divine.

A note was handed to Huber at the front office, and it read, "Executive Chef Keith Moretti, will meet with you on the promenade deck mid-starboard side, tomorrow morning, Friday, June 22, at 11:30."

"That was easy!" Huber said. Then she winked at Andi and asked, "Are you ready to shoot craps?"

"I thought you'd never ask!" Andi replied, and they headed for the Casino on deck two.

CHAPTER 34

Keith Moretti's curiosity was aroused when summoned to have a talk with a female passenger named R. A. Huber. He did a Google search linking him to her website. A private eye, he thought, wondering what she wanted. Was it possible that he still had an outstanding gambling debt? He probed his mind in vain, trying to come up with a reason for an investigation.

There were two women waiting for him on the promenade deck; one older and elegant, the other young and a looker with wild red hair and long legs. As he approached, the senior took charge.

She said, "Thanks for making time for us, Mr. Moretti. I'm R. A. Huber and this is Antoinette LeJeune. First off, let me compliment you on an excellent job as executive chef. The food on this ship is superb. You must be in charge of a small army of chefs!"

As they made themselves comfortable on the deck chairs fitted with multi-colored striped cushions, Keith wrinkled up his forehead and said, "If you wanted to praise the cooking and the managing of chefs in my galley, a simple note would have sufficed. So what's this all about?"

"We are private investigators."

"I know. I looked you up. What do you want from me?"

"We are investigating the murder of your brother."

He stared in disbelieve and then asked, "Didn't Rachel do it?"

"We were hired to clear her."

"Good luck!"

"You feel certain of her guilt?"

"It seems a logical conclusion under the circumstances, don't you think?"

Huber studied his features. They were chiseled as if carved out of wood, with a generous forehead above a straight, narrow nose. His hair and eyes were dark brown.

She recalled the "In Memoriam" picture of Steven she saw on the Cucina di Enzo website during her initial research of the company and said, "You resemble your brother."

Keith said, "He was far better looking." And giving her a scrutinizing glance, he asked, "Did you meet Steve?"

"No, I only saw a photo of him." And she remarked, "I note that you and Bart Trimboli refer to him as Steve, but for everyone else I've talked to he was Steven."

"That's what we called him as kids, and even when we became adults I still called him Steve, whether he liked it or not." And he added, "So you've talked to Bart."

"I sure did, and he shared how he loved to play with you Moretti boys as youngsters."

"Good old Bart!"

"I'd like to get your perspective of what growing up in your family was like."

Keith shrugged and said, "I was an average kid, stuck between a domineering brain of a bro and a musically gifted baby sis."

Andi put in, "I reckon that ruffled your feathers some."

Amused by her Southern drawl he replied, "You could say that! It was irritating to be in the shadow of Mister Popularity. Steve excelled at sports, got straight A's, and our neighborhood friends followed him like lambs. As teens, I knew better than to bring any girlfriend home for fear that he'd snatch her away." And with a boyish grin he said, "But being mediocre had advantages. No one, including my parents, expected much of me."

Huber probed, "How would you describe your relationship with your brother on an adult level?"

There was that boyish smirk again as Keith answered, "I know where you're going with this. I'm sure you've learned that I had a fight with Steve and left town."

"Yes, that came to my attention. I don't know the details but learned that you had a disagreement and opted to leave the company."

"Well, I won't tell you the details either, but it turned out that, as always, he was right. As a matter of fact, Cucina di Enzo kept prospering under his leadership. My bro could do no wrong."

"The restaurant chain aside, how did you get along personally?"

"Steve objected to my gambling, big time. As for me, I didn't approve of his hitting on every female within a 20-mile radius. Other than that, we got along fine."

Huber said, "So after your dispute, you sought employment with this cruise line company and have been executive chef on one of their ships for the last two-and-a-half years?"

"Not right away. I first moved to Las Vegas, where I started my own restaurant."

Huber queried, "And that didn't work out?"

Embarrassed, he admitted, "I lost the restaurant because of my gambling addiction." And he quickly added, "I have it under control now; haven't seen the inside of a casino in over a year and never go near the gambling hall on the ship."

"Good for you!" she said, and Andi gave him thumbs up.

"Most people have no idea what it is like to overcome a compulsion."

Huber said, "Believe me, I know! I was addicted to nicotine and quitting smoking turned out to be the hardest thing I ever did." Then she went on with the interview and mentioned, "Jennifer's drowning and your attempt to save her must have been a horrendous experience."

He shot back, "I don't want to talk about it. Bart had no business bringing it up."

"Actually, I first learned about your sister's drowning accident from your father. Bart only discussed the tragedy after I prompted him on it. I can see that the subject is still too painful for you. Let's talk about Rachel."

"I hardly know her," he replied. "We met at Dad's house last Christmas, and then I saw her one more time at Steve's housewarming party."

"What was your impression of her?"

"She seemed nice. Hard to believe she poisoned Steve."

"But you *do* believe it?"

"Jealousy is a sickness and must have driven her to it. I guess the oleander bush in the yard happened to be at her convenience."

"Speaking of that bush, did you hear the remark she made about it while giving a tour of the property?"

"Sure. It struck me as funny at the time, but after Steve died of oleander poisoning exactly the way she predicted, her comment turned to doom."

"When did you make peace with your brother?"

"I first wrote him a long letter last September when he got engaged, basically telling him that he had been right and admitting that I overreacted on the day I called it quits and stormed out of the board meeting. We officially made up in person last Christmas." There was pain in his eyes as he said, "Now I'm really glad that we did."

"How did you first learn of Steven's death?"

"I was on the Australia/New Zealand route – Auckland/Sidney – for two weeks and just sailing into its end-port harbor of Sidney in the early evening of April 9 when Dad called with the news."

Andi asked, "He couldn't get ahold of you until the next day?"

"Oh, he called right away. Sidney is approximately 20 hours ahead of California, so when Dad called from San Diego on the night of April 8, we were already at April 9 in Australia."

"How dumb of me," Andi said with an apologetic smile.

He went on, "I was scheduled to do a reverse run – Sidney/Auckland – but instead flew home for Steve's funeral."

Huber said, "Dealing with Steven's death must be especially hard for your dad, given his illness."

"What illness?" Keith shouted in astonishment, causing a couple who passed by to stare at him.

Huber for her part was taken aback and asked, "You don't know that he has pancreatic cancer?"

Keith shook his head. Then he murmured, "So that's why he looked so awful at the funeral. I thought it was from grief."

As if on cue, Huber and Andi averted their glances away from Keith and out to sea, giving him time to adjust to this bad piece of news. Andi pointed to a couple of seagulls fluttering by, and within another second they were out of sight.

Keith broke the silence and said, "In that case I may go home earlier and spend some time with Dad."

"When did you plan to see him next?"

"Not until Thanksgiving or Christmas, but now I'm thinking August, as he may need my support during Rachel's trial."

"Good idea!"

"I'm about ready to give up the vagabond life anyway and settle down."

"Is there any chance you're considering rejoining the family business?"

"Nope. They paid me out when I quit, and I no longer have any claim on the company. If you're suggesting that I could ever take Steve's place, you're way off. I'm not qualified nor would I want the responsibility. I am a cook and perfectly happy to stay a cook."

"Who will inherit Cucina de Enzo, Incorporated, after your father passes on?"

"I have no idea," he replied. "Possibly Marco or maybe it will be sold."

"You are related to Marco Valente, correct?"

"Only distantly, but that didn't prevent Dad from taking him in for a while as a kid when his old man did time."

"Oh?"

"I'd assumed you did a background check on Marco and knew about his dad."

"No, I didn't."

"Valente senior got cozy with the mob and his wife took off to Sicily when they put him in jail. Dad gave Marco a home during the one-year prison term."

"That was kind and generous of him."

They were interrupted by the captain's announcement over the loudspeakers: "We are approaching the port of Juneau. Passengers, please get ready to disembark in one hour."

As they got to their feet, Keith said, "I need to look after things in the galley before we dock. If there are more questions, you know where to find me."

"I think we've covered it all. Thank you, Mr. Moretti."

He gave them both a short nod, turned on his heels, and disappeared farther down the deck.

Huber looked at Andi and said, "So much for business. Now let's get ready to explore Juneau."

CHAPTER 35

In the early afternoon they stepped on the bus to experience "The Best of Juneau" on their combination tour, starting at the Mendenhall Glacier Visitor Center to see Alaska's best-known river of ice. Huber took numerous photos of it from different angles, and then they decided to hike down the wooded path for a closer look at the glacier. The weather in these parts of the world was known to change from one minute to the next. When they set off on the trail, the sky had become overcast, and as they headed back, it started to rain. By the time they returned to the Visitor Center, it poured, and they got soaked despite their umbrellas and ponchos.

The motor coach ride then took them to scenic Auke Bay - - unfortunately it was hard to make out the scenic part through the downpour - - where they boarded a water-jet-powered catamaran specifically designed for wildlife viewing. They dried off in the warm, comfortable cabin surrounded by large windows as they explored the island-studded waters of Stephens Passage. The captain of the boat explained that the area was a favored summer feeding ground for humpback whales. He announced, "Once whales have been sighted, I will maneuver the catamaran to allow viewing and photo opportunities."

Andi turned to Huber and said, "You reckon the rain is goin' to spook them?"

"I doubt that they'll care; they're already wet!" Huber replied with a grin.

The captain spoke into the microphone, "A sighting at 6:00 was spotted!" Everyone cranked their heads in the direction of the stern. Moments later he pointed out, "Look between 9:00 and 10:00 and you'll see another one!" The numbers, of course, corresponded to the location as seen on a clock. He cut down the motor and idled at a low pace.

Suddenly, their vessel was surrounded by numerous other small boats, all waiting expectantly to see more whales. Andi was scrutinizing the waters through binoculars provided by the boat tour, while Huber, seated at the port window, happened to glance immediately in front of her and witnessed a blowing with the naked eye, about ten yards away. A moment later, apparently the same whale surfaced on their starboard side in a spectacular breach. People on the boat clapped and yelped in excitement. They sighted a few more whales, but nothing proved as exhilarating as having observed that graceful ocean giant slowly arc his massive tail into the air.

They stepped ashore at Orca Point Lodge on Colt Island to a feast of fresh grilled wild Alaska salmon, rice pilaf, corn on the cob, coleslaw, and dessert. Since it was still raining hard, they skipped the stroll along the beach before the return boat ride to Auke Bay.

At "home" on the cruise ship that evening, they settled into the Explorer's Lounge, sipping champagne and listening to a violin and piano duo of two young women performing classical music.

Andi remarked, "That chick knows how to work a fiddle!"

"She certainly does," Huber agreed.

By the time their ship sailed at 11:00, they called it a night since they needed to get up early the next morning for their land excursion in Skagway.

CHAPTER 36

Huber did not sleep well. She heard the fog horn all through the night. The disturbing sound did not seem to bother Andi a bit. The young woman's regular breathing was testimony that she slept soundly through it.

At the crack of dawn Andi woke up, went out on the balcony and hollered, "The fog is so thick, you could play hide'n seek in it."

"You go ahead and do that," Huber murmured, turned to her other side, and went back to sleep.

At nine o'clock, when they stepped on the tour bus in Skagway, the fog had lifted and the promise of a sunny day lay ahead. They ascended into the beautiful White Pass Mountains as their tour guide shared the history of the Klondike Gold Rush. They spotted a mountain goat high up on a ridge, standing perfectly still like a statue. Then something alerted the animal and it took off, jumping from rock to rock, and soon vanished from view.

The motor coach stopped at the US border, where a border control officer entered the vehicle and checked all passengers' passports. "Checking" them is an exaggeration; people on board had their passports open at the photo page and the officer gave each a quick glance as he moved to the rear of the bus and back. In Fraser, British Columbia, they switched onto the White Pass & Yukon Route Railroad and boarded an old-fashioned narrow-gauge train. Huber and Andi sat in the caboose. Now it was the Canadian official's turn to glance at their passports. Making their way down the pass on the opposite side of the Yukon River, they took in the sights of Tormented Valley and Pitchfork Falls.

As the train weaved around curves, Huber got a good view of the locomotive and middle cars, snapping several pictures, and when they neared and were about to pass over what looked like a bridge built centuries ago, she wondered if the old structure would hold.

Andi suddenly yelled, "Look!" and pointed down the ravine. To Huber's delight, she was able to spot a black mama bear with her cub thrashing about the edge of the river, before her view was blocked by forest trees.

At the foot of the pass, next to a waterfall, they visited Liarsville Gold Rush Trail Camp, where they enjoyed a delicious lunch of wild Alaskan salmon, barbecued on an open pit. There followed a little show, staged by a cast of miners and dancehall girls, all about lies and lying, appropriate for a place called Liarsville.

Back in Skagway, they visited the historic world-famous Red Onion Saloon and brothel. The brothel museum had obviously some ladies of the night images and content, as well as the priceless silver dress worn by the Onion's first Madam, and many other original artifacts left by the "soiled doves."

The guided tour ended at this point, and they were left to stroll around the picturesque town at their leisure. The main drag consisted of mostly jewelry stores and souvenir shops. Neither Huber nor Andi felt like shopping, so they went for a swift walk away from the tourist hustle and bustle before returning to their ship. The wind had picked up by that time, blowing at about 50 miles an hour, so that they had to fight it every step of the way.

After dinner that night, they saw a show with the cruise liner's talented singers and dancers. It was superb! The performance could easily compete with any acclaimed Broadway show.

CHAPTER 37

On the next day, Sunday, June 24, their ship did not go on land but cruised all day. They glided past emerald forests and through pristine fjords, past Strawberry Island, Willoughby Island, navigating the Whidbey Passage to glorious Glacier Bay. The sheer wonder of the legendary Glacier Bay National Park in its immense beauty took their breath away.

In the late afternoon, Huber and Andi admired the scene from their balcony as the ship passed in close vicinity of the face of numerous glaciers. Without warning, and right in front of their eyes, they were treated to the drama of a calving glacier.

"Holly Krewe!" Andi exclaimed, as glacier pieces broke and dropped into the ocean in a spectacular show of nature.

Huber said, "Nothing can top that! Let's start getting ready for our second and last formal dinner. I'll shower first."

They had settled into their stateroom for the night and Andi remarked, "What an excitin' day!"

"It sure was," Huber agreed. "Watching the calving of a glacier at close range doesn't happen every day!"

Then she said, "Ready for some shop talk?"

"About motives?"

"That and whatever else comes to mind," Huber replied.

She reached for her iPad and brought up the notes of the Rachel Penrose file she had downloaded at home, saying, "Let's first talk about the victim in order to get clues about possible motives. Here is Steven's portrait as painted by people I've interviewed: The person who hired me, Rachel's friend, Dr. Jonathan Lighthart, hardly knew him but shared his opinion of the man." Glancing at her notes, she quoted, "'My impression of him was that of an aggressive man, always taking what he wanted.' Rachel did not want to talk about Steven at all yet managed to give me an account of what fun they'd had skiing Mammoth when they met for the first time. His father talked about how things always came easy to his eldest, and that he had a knack for turning every happening to his own advantage. His childhood friend Bart said he was a born leader and easy to get along with as long as he called the shots.

"Steven's exotic dancer friend did not mince words and called him a stud with tons of money who knew how to dress and converse, but deep down he'd been nothing more than a calculating jerk. The new CEO at Cucina di Enzo, Incorporated, described him as a genius, and the female board member remembered her late boss as being brilliant and a clever manipulator. She was also impressed with him as a man - -" Huber consulted her notes again "- - she thought him 'drop-dead gorgeous.'"

She continued, "I didn't write this down, but as I recall Tina and Shane Brook found him entertaining. Zack, his would-be best man, described Steven with one word: success. And lastly, you heard for yourself what Keith told us about his brother."

"Sure thing, boss. He said Steven was a whiz but also bossy, which pissed him off when growing up." And she remarked, "You left out the housekeeper and the other guy from Cucina di Enzo."

"Good, Andi, you're paying attention to detail! I guess the reason Kevin Gasparian slipped my mind is because he didn't seem to have an opinion of Steven Moretti, or didn't want to voice it. He also made it clear that he had no interest in his fellow board of directors' personalities or their private lives. Rufina Ramos, on the other hand, made a profound statement. Even though she claimed not to have known her employer of four years well, she had the interesting opinion that the man liked himself way too much to commit suicide."

Huber looked up from her iPad and said, "That our victim was an excellent businessman goes without saying, but what else have we learned from all these people?"

Andi replied, "That he was a good-looking SOB, always gettin' what he wanted, be it women or professional success."

"Right. And what stood out for me when talking with these folks is that, with maybe the exception of his dad, nobody seemed grief-stricken by his death. Steven Moretti may have been a man admired, respected, envied, and hated, but not loved."

Andi said, "Rachel must've loved him and then her love turned to hate."

"You remember my famous three basic types of murder motives, not counting street crimes and gang violence?"

"Yes, ma'am: greed, passion, and self-preservation."

"Let's put our suspects into their respective categories. Steven's father and brother, and also Marco Valente, would qualify for 'greed.' A passion crime would obviously apply to Rachel Penrose, and we have to include Jonathan Lighthart, Jasmine Dewitt, Claudia Chambers, and

possibly Zack Jefferson in the passion grouping.   Bart
Trimboli, Rufina Ramos, Kevin Gasparian and the Brook
couple are harder to categorize. All suspects could have
acted in self-preservation to conceal a former crime or
secret."

Surprised, Andi asked, "Why did you add his father
and even Rachel's doctor friend to the list of suspects?"

"It is unlikely that Mr. Enzo Moretti killed his son,
especially given his physical condition, but you know
my rule of never excluding anyone. The fact is that the
senior Moretti is now the sole owner of the Cucina di
Enzo enterprise. As for Jonathan Lighthart, it is true that
he hired me to clear Rachel, and I am 100% positive that
he wants me to succeed, but he could have committed the
crime himself. Don't forget, he is in love with her even if
she is unaware of it."

Neither spoke for a while. Andi mulled over what her
boss had pointed out and Huber revisited in her mind the
conversations she had had with each person of interest.

Andi finally spoke up and said, "I'm stuck on the gain
mode. It's possible that the Valente guy ends up with the
Cucina di Enzo business, but Keith has no more claim to it,
so why do you put him in the 'greed' group?"

"You are correct; Keith does not inherit the company.
I've known that ever since my interview with his father.
I'm thinking of Steven's private estate. As far as we know,
he didn't make a will, and I think that his dad inherits
most of Steven's private assets. Now remember, Keith
didn't seem to know that Mr. Moretti, Sr., has terminal
cancer, and of course that makes him less of a suspect in
the greed department, but I aim to make sure he told the
truth before I cross him of that category."

"I don't get it! What does Mr. Moretti's cancer have to
do with it?"

"The man is only 64 and would normally have a life expectancy of another 15 years or more."

"Of course!" Andi exclaimed. "So Keith would have to wait a long time to get his money or have to kill his daddy too."

Then she said, "Another dumb question. Why did you put Zack Jefferson in the 'passion' group?"

"Admittedly, it happened a long time ago, but Steven did steal his girlfriend and Zack may have still held a grudge, waiting for an opportunity to act on it."

Andi proposed, "Since Steven was such a dynamo with women, you figure he slept with others besides the stripper?"

"I'd answer that with a definitive yes."

"So some of the guys you tagged as 'hard to categorize' would fit into the 'passion' group as jealous husbands."

Huber closed her iPad and, tapping it, remarked, "I'd say that leaves us with plenty of food for thought."

Before they turned off the light that night, Huber said, "Sorry that we don't get good phone reception up here. I know that you miss talking to Bo. Feel free to use my iPad if you want to send him an e-mail message."

"That's okay. I can't get ahold of him this week anyhow. He's on the road to South Carolina, helping his sister move."

"Sometimes taking a break in a relationship is a good thing."

"How so?"

"I'm sure you've heard the phrase 'Absence makes the heart grow fonder.'"

CHAPTER 38

The next day, Huber and Andi set out for their "Best of Ketchikan by Land & Sea" tour. Seated on the bus, they were driven through the picturesque town with multi-colored houses. Their driver/guide pointed out historic Creek Street, where homes and shops were perched over the water on wooden pilings.

They stopped at Saxman Totem Village to view one of the world's largest groupings of totems. Their guide interpreted the meaning of the giant sentries that bordered the park. Then their sightseeing continued to George Inlet, where a stroll through the rainforest brought them to the historic Libby Cannery. Yes, indeed, the Alaskan forests more than qualified as rainforests, their yearly rain averaging 12 feet!

The local Libby Cannery was founded in 1914 and remained in operation until 1958. They were shown a short video, taking them back to the days when rugged men and women toiled day and night to harvest and process the abundant Alaska salmon catch. Then they toured the place and saw the historic Tsirku Canning Line and were told that it was the only functioning equipment of its kind left in the world.

From the cannery dock, they boarded a water-jet-powered vessel for wildlife viewing along the coastline of glacier-carved George Inlet. These waterways were surrounded by rainforest. They spotted a bald eagle and his nest at the crown of a tall tree. The catamaran was kept at low speed for a few minutes in case there were any whale sightings, but the majestic animals were not cooperating. They did not see a single whale.

Once back on board ship, there was ample time for them to get a bit physical. Huber first jogged around the promenade deck a couple of times and then went to watch Andi in the pool area on the Lido deck, where she was one of the finalists in the Ping-Pong tournament. Andi ended up in third place, and her prize was a T-shirt with the cruise liner's logo.

After dinner they saw a magic show, and when they walked away from that performance in the Vista Lounge, they both agreed that the magician could easily hold his own with any of the popular illusionists currently dazzling a Las Vegas strip audience.

While their ship cruised the Inside Passage once again on its way to Vancouver, a good part of the sleuths' last day on board was taken up by packing and filling out forms. They enjoyed the food, comfort and entertainment of their moving "home" one more time.

On Wednesday, June 27, their disembarkation took place with as much efficiency as had their embarkation a week earlier. Before going to bed the night before, all luggage except carry-ons had to be placed outside peoples' staterooms no later than 1:00 a.m. During the night, capable ship personnel removed the bags from the hallways for transport to the airport. Early in the morning, passengers gathered into groups according to their predestined colors and numbers. Huber and Andi's was "Red 3" and as soon as the color "red" was announced over the loudspeaker, they made their way to the designated meeting place, where they showed passport and ship-card credentials and were escorted out of the ship to a waiting bus, transporting them to the Vancouver airport. Their luggage was waiting for them at the terminal.

At home Huber told Peter that the Alaskan cruise had been even more adventurous than expected and that she and Andi had had a great time.

"So what did you see?" he wanted to know.

"Lots of wildlife: humpback whales, black bears, bald eagles, and even a mountain goat. But the highlight of the entire trip was seeing a glacier calving right in front of us!"

Peter asked, "What about the main purpose of your voyage?"

Huber became somber and said, "That's a disappointment. Although we learned some interesting new facts from the talk with Keith Moretti, they do not bring me any closer to getting at the truth about Steven's murder."

CHAPTER 39

On Saturday afternoon, June 30, Andi decided to pay Bo a surprise visit, figuring that he'd be back from moving his sister out to California. Summer had arrived and was here to stay. Andi welcomed the gentle breeze upon her face as she rode her Harley-Davidson from Santa Monica, where she shared an apartment with two other UCLA students, over to the San Fernando Valley.

As always, the 405 Freeway was busy – weekend or not – but traffic eased when she made the transition to the 118, and once she got onto the 210, had a free run. Exiting the freeway and nearing Bo's street, she could hardly contain her excitement. The remodeling of his home would either be finished or nearly so. She couldn't wait to see it and, most of all, to rush into Bo's arms. Andi pictured his look of astonishment when hearing the sound of her bike, and then he'd come running to greet her as she'd pull up by the house.

His truck was not in the driveway and neither was his Harley. Instead, there was a white Mazda sedan parked on it.

Andi left her bike on the street, walked to the front door, and rang the bell.

A pretty woman opened the door and said, "Yes?" And a girl of about seven or eight appeared by her side, asking, "Who is it, Momma?"

"I'm Andi. Is Bo around?"

"He's running an errand and should be back any moment."

Starting to extend her hand, Andi said, "You must be his sister. Nice to meet ya."

"He doesn't have a sister. I'm his wife."

As if stung by a bee, Andi pulled her hand back and stared. Then she managed to say, "Sorry," turned her back to the woman and child, donned her helmet, and then bolted to her bike.

Bo's wife called after her, "Wait! Are you his client? Want me to give him a message?"

Andi was already in the saddle and shook her head. Then she kicked the kickstand up, hit the starter button, put her machine into gear, and sped away. Her world had come crashing down in a matter of seconds. Nothing seemed real; her ears were ringing, the heart was racing, and she couldn't see straight. The road turned into a blur, and surprisingly she found her way home, weaving around cars at a speed of 75 miles an hour. Miraculously, she made it to Santa Monica without causing an accident or being stopped and ticketed by a police officer.

She reached the apartment and fumbled for her keys, eventually getting the door open with a trembling hand. Then she sprinted to the bathroom, barely missing a collision with her roommate, who came out of the kitchen carrying a glass of wine in one hand and balancing a stack of books in the other.

Andi locked herself into the bathroom, kneeled in front of the toilet and retched. Then she put the lid down, sat on it, and cried her heart out.

CHAPTER 40

In order to verify a couple of things, Huber opted to have another talk with Enzo Moretti. He picked up on the third ring and his "Hello" sounded weak.

She stated her name and he said, "I know," obviously having checked the caller I.D. on his phone.

Huber inquired, "How are you doing, Mr. Moretti?"

"Taking one day at a time."

"I just came back from an Alaskan cruise and met with your son Keith."

"How was it?"

"Absolutely breath-taking! Have you done it?"

"I meant to, but a cruise is not feasible for me now."

She regretted her question and hoped not to stir up more sad emotion with the next comment she was about to make. "I'm afraid that I let the cat out of the bag when I mentioned your illness to Keith. I didn't realize that you kept it a secret from your family."

He took his time before he answered, "I hated the thought of them worrying and fussing over me. Steven pressured me into telling him, though, at the last board meeting when he noticed that I looked sick. I made him promise not to let Keith know."

"I'm sorry." And she remarked, "Keith sure seems to see the world; Australia, New Zealand, and now Alaska."

Mr. Moretti said, "And that's not all by far. Before the Australian run, for instance, he did a few Western Caribbean round trips out of Fort Lauderdale, Florida. The big draw for him to this particular cruise company was that they'd send him on different routes."

Then Huber said, "You were extremely generous by giving Marco Valente a home for a year."

"So Keith told you about that. It wasn't the boy's fault that his family became dysfunctional."

"Still, making him your responsibility was an act of kindness."

"He blended in well with us. Giuseppa and I missed him after he went back to his own folks when his father's prison term ended and his mother decided to come back from Italy."

"Well, you've maintained a lasting relationship. He joined your workforce."

"True, and he's been a great support to me ever since Steven died. Even before he kept in touch, but lately he calls and makes the trip to San Diego more often."

Huber felt certain that the talk had tired him and ended the call.

CHAPTER 41

A few days went by and summer hit with a vengeance by the beginning of July. The temperature climbed to triple digits, making Huber grateful to be sitting out the heat wave in her air-conditioned office. The heat wasn't the only thing bothering her. The Rachel Penrose investigation had come to a standstill, making her pressured for time.

Determined to get results, she went through the process of revisiting in her mind every interview she'd conducted and each location she came across since starting the investigation. About to give up, she suddenly formed a mental picture of a row of oleander bushes. The image was so real and precise that it gave her a jolt. "Bingo!" she said aloud, remembering exactly where she had seen those plants

And then Keith's words came back to her: "Jealousy is a sickness." Yes, of course, she told herself. I looked at the crime from the wrong angle. She stared into space for some time, contemplating her new theory. Then she consulted her file, scrutinizing her entries once more, paying specific attention to dates. Yes, she concluded, it all fits.

She jumped into action. First she needed to contact Tea Brewer in England to verify that they had shipped a loose leaf tea order to a certain person in the US, and if so, when that order was processed. Huber decided to make the request in a formal letter by regular mail. Then she composed an e-mail and sent it to all people involved. It read:

"I have a good lead concerning a possible solution to Steven Moretti's homicide. This murder plot goes deeper than at first glance. I've uncovered a dark secret. And here is another hint: There are many places besides Steven's backyard where oleander bushes are grown. I happen to believe that I know where the killer found the oleander leaves that were added to the victim's tea."

Her initial plan was to send the e-mail only to her main suspect, but she changed her mind and sent it to all, her reasoning being that she may learn from comments of the innocent too. Plus she had to accept the possibility that she could be wrong in her assumption.

Jonathan Lighthart called right away and said, "So whose dark secret? And where are those oleander bushes?" She had to tell him that she wasn't ready to give out that information yet. Most others did not respond to her message at all, save for a few e-mails ranging from, "Can you be more specific?" to "Good for you." Her main suspect had not yet taken the bait. She could only hope that he eventually would react to her intimation. Meanwhile, she would wait for the response from Tea Brewer.

On the next day, when an insurance company sought her services in a jewelry theft claim they suspected of being fraudulent, she accepted the case, since she never liked to be idle.

CHAPTER 42

By the time the response letter from Tea Brewer arrived in the mail, the date was already August 1. They confirmed that a tea shipment to the person Huber indicated had been processed on March 14. The parcel was mailed to a PO Box and should have reached the recipient in the United States around March 21 to 24. Huber did an online search and thought, good! Now I know for sure who the murderer is. Proving it will be another matter, and time is running out.

She called Andi and first asked, "Have I told you how sorry I am about Bo?"

"I don't remember," Andi replied. "I'll get over him."

"Did he ever try to explain?"

"Sure thing. He's called, texted, and sent a long e-mail. I haven't answered any of it."

"But you've read his e-mail?"

"Of course! He told some humbug story of how they'd had marital problems and that his wife and daughter had moved back with her kinfolk while they sorted things out. And he went into the usual crap of having fallen in love with me at first sight when we met at the Harley dealer. He also wrote that he meant to tell me about his marriage but never found the right moment. All bullshit. I wonder how long he was gonna string me along. I feel sorry for his wife; she seemed nice."

Huber said, "Telling you that he helped move his sister to California when in reality he went to fetch his wife from South Carolina makes him a coward. And he timed it conveniently with you safely tucked away on a cruise."

"No jivin'!"

There was a long pause on the line, making Huber think that they had lost the connection. Then Andi exploded, "He made me feel special, and now it turns out I was only his dirty little whore."

"There is nothing dirty or little about you, Andi. Don't degrade yourself."

Andi changed the subject and asked, "How are we doin' in the Rachel Penrose case?"

"I just received a letter from Tea Brewer, confirming my suspicion. The dates pan out too."

"That's great news! We know our villain now."

"You and I do, but how are we going to prove it?"

"Sure thing, boss, the killer ordered and received the tea shipment, and the rest is easy as pie to figure out."

"It's not against the law to order tea from the same company as the victim did. And by the same token, I'm positive that I know where the poisonous oleander leaves that were added to Steven's tea came from, but cannot prove it. The motive of the crime is clear to me too, and again, I have no hard evidence to support my claim. No, Andi, we need to come up with more than we've got. Let's put our heads together tomorrow and hope for a brainstorm."

At home that evening, Peter became aware of his spouse's frustration and suggested, "Why don't you go to

Rachel's attorney and give him all the information you've gathered and let him worry about the rest?"

Regula replied, "I may have no other choice. David Wachterman has listed me as a witness to testify at the trial and wants to go over the testimony with me. Andi and I are scheduled to meet in his office next Monday. Still, I'd like to have a stronger case against my suspect. In order to set things right, I need to convince the jury that my theory is the only acceptable one. The problem is that all my evidence is circumstantial."

Peter said, "Sleep on it; you'll come up with something."

"Easy for you to say."

Then he remarked, "Today is the 1st of August. I'm sorry that I can't go to the *Ersten August Feier* at the Swiss Park in Whittier on Sunday."

"That's right; your Writers Conference in Santa Barbara is this weekend. When are you leaving?"

"Friday morning. I'd like to amble around town and stroll on the pier before the conference starts. And what are you up to while I'm gone?"

"Now that you remind me of the Swiss National Day, I may drive to Whittier for the August *Feier*. And on Friday, Peggy and I have a date to play a round of golf. Haven't seen her in ages; we are overdue. Besides, a change of scenery might do me good."

She glanced his way and noticed his amused expression. "What?"

"I've been thinking. One of the reasons our marriage has lasted so long is that we enjoy doing things together but are equally comfortable with pursuing our interests separately."

"And here I thought it was because of my irresistible charm!"

"That too!"

CHAPTER 43

Early Friday morning, August 3, Steven Moretti's killer parked three houses away from the Huber residence. He had been stalking R. A. Huber since Monday of that week, and the fruitless effort started to wear on him. He needed to find a way to get at her before the trial, and the clock kept ticking. He felt justified taking some extra time off, considering that silencing Huber would save his neck. Trailing her had been easy, despite her unlisted home address. The woman had a state-of-the-art website with pictures of herself and her assistant and, most important, the location of her office.

The surveillance so far had been routine. An attack near her office was out of the question. The small place was at ground level of a two-story office building, wedged between other business offices on either side, and faced the parking lot. Equipped with a burglar alarm, the office had only one door to get in and out. At the end of the day on Monday, the villain had followed his prey from her office in Pasadena to her home in Merida in a dark blue rented Honda Accord. Her house stood in a well-cared-for neighborhood with manicured lawns and looked secure. He couldn't risk breaking in for fear of an alarm going off.

On Tuesday morning, he took up the tail again from Merida and tracked her to the gym. He found a space in the busy parking lot a good distance away from where she had found a spot and watched her get out of her car. She wore running shorts and carried a tote bag with a racquet handle sticking out of it at one end. I doubt that they have indoor tennis courts here, the killer thought. She must play racquet ball. But without a gym membership, he could not follow her into the building, so he waited. An hour and a half later, Huber reappeared in a turquoise summer dress and open-toed pumps, walked to her car, and drove out of the parking lot.

The culprit dropped the newspaper he was hiding behind and chased after her. He let another car get between them as they merged onto the 210 Freeway east, and when she exited on Lake Avenue, he knew where she was headed. He watched her turn into the parking area of her office building but kept going. No need to pursue her further. She would most likely stay there for the rest of the day.

To be on the safe side, he exchanged the rental Honda for a silver Chevrolet Malibu on Wednesday, and Huber led him to her office where she stayed all day. In the evening, she drove back to Merida, where her stalker didn't bother to take the exit leading to her residence but resumed his surveillance the next morning. When she drove to her gym again on Thursday, he skipped tailing her into its parking lot and went to have breakfast at a coffee shop. Later, he checked the parking spaces by her office to make sure he hadn't missed an opportunity.

As expected, her car was there. He circled the lot a couple of times, undecided whether to stay or call it quits for the day, as a motorcyclist pulled into a spot, parked the bike, and took off the helmet, causing unruly red hair to spread over her leather jacket. So Huber's sidekick is riding a Harley-Davidson. Interesting! He decided to stay, on the slim possibility that the two women would guide him somewhere useful. After over an hour the young woman came out of Huber's office alone and rode off on her motorcycle. When the villain realized that the senior sleuth stayed put, he gave up and drove away.

At last, on Friday, the murderer got his lucky break. He looked on as the door to R. A. Huber's residence opened and her husband kissed her good-bye at the threshold, walked over to his SUV parked on the driveway, stashed his small suitcase inside, and took off. Aha! Hubby is going out of town, the observer thought. A short time later, Huber drove out of the attached garage. He waited until she made it to the end of the block and turned into the cross street before starting the Malibu. He caught up to her just before reaching the onramp to the 210 Freeway going east. He anticipated another wasted day of seeing her drive to work, when she made the transition to the Glendale Freeway instead of continuing toward Pasadena.

She exited on Holly Drive, made the loop around to East Glenoaks Boulevard, and then drove along many blocks of a residential neighborhood. He kept his distance with two cars between them. They passed an open gate with a signpost announcing, *Welcome to Snake Canyon Golf & Tennis,* and then the curvy road wound up the mountain in a steady climb until they reached the golf course entrance.

Huber found a parking space close to the clubhouse, and her adversary opted to leave his car farther away but had a clear view of her. He stayed put while she took her gear out of the trunk, attached her golf bag to the push cart, and changed her shoes. He watched as she donned a visor, stored a bottle of water in the long pocket of her golf bag, locked her car and placed the keys into the small front pocket of the bag. Then she walked toward the clubhouse and vanished from view.

The suspect got out of the Malibu and strolled toward the structure, hiding behind oversized sunglasses and a baseball cap pulled way down into the face. Standing near the practice putting green, pretending to watch a guy perfect his puts, he saw Huber embrace another woman in a bear hug. Then the two left their golf bags unattended and walked, chatting non-stop, in the direction of the ladies room.

Here came his chance! He quickly went to Huber's bag, unzipped its front pocket and grabbed her keys. He made himself walk at a normal pace while passing by the clubhouse window but started sprinting as soon as it was out of sight. He clicked the door open even before reaching Huber's car. Once inside, he checked the glove compartment. He had guessed right; he found her garage door opener in it. The killer snatched it up, relocked the car, and ran back to Huber's bag. No one paid any attention as he nonchalantly returned the keys to their proper place. Seconds later, Huber and her friend Peggy left the bathroom and came around the corner of the building, but all they saw was the antagonist's back as he slowly walked away.

CHAPTER 44

R. A. Huber drove home and reminisced on what a perfect day she'd had. In order to be done before the temperature would climb to the nineties, they had teed off early. The view from Snake Canyon Golf Course generated a feeling of being king of the world, looking down over the city of Los Angeles to one side, and Glendale to the other. On a clear day, one could even get a glimpse of the ocean.

Their scores had been less than impressive and her friend Peggy never took the sport seriously, but they'd had lots of laughs. Peggy stood barely 5'2" tall but oh, what a fireball! The flamboyant extrovert had changed her hairstyle and color again, this time sporting a short, strawberry-blond do that went well with her light complexion and baby blue eyes. Peggy was fun to be with, no matter what the occasion. She had a way of seeing the comical side of things. On the back nine, when losing her third ball down the canyon, instead of getting angry, she giggled and said, "Another one bites the dust!"

They had lunched on the clubhouse patio and caught up on each other's lives. After a bragging session of their respective grandkids' accomplishments, Peggy complained about her husband Walt, who was recently retired and bored. The way Peggy put it, "He bugs the heck out of me, keeping at my heels like a puppy dog." Huber smiled to herself when she thought of the advice she'd given her friend: "Get him a dog of his own; that ought to keep him busy."

She had stopped at her office to take care of snail mail and, arriving in Merida, swung by the grocery store since they were out of everything. Her trunk space was taken up with golf stuff, so she placed the three grocery bags on the floor behind the front seats. Huber had refused to let the Rachel Penrose investigation enter her mind all day, and it felt good.

Now, nearing home, the case crept back into her consciousness. Why had the killer not reacted to her e-mail? she mused. The messages hadn't been sent out as a group. She had taken the trouble to address each one individually, so he must have thought he was the sole recipient. She had expected him to either try to divert her attention to someone else or at least feel her out for how much she knew. The person must be aware that her testimony at the trial could have grave consequences. Getting the silent treatment left her disappointed. Or was the murderer too smart to play her game, and might he strike without warning? She resolved to carry her pistol from here on out, starting tomorrow.

Huber arrived at her house and reached for the garage door opener. It wasn't in the glove compartment where she'd left it in the morning. How strange! She searched between the seats and under them, to no avail. I can't believe it. Must have been a senior moment, she thought. I'll look for it later. Right now, I need to put the groceries in the fridge before the milk turns sour. She parked in the driveway, grabbed two bags from the back of her sedan, leaving the door open to fetch the third later, and walked to the front entrance. With her hands full, she struggled to get the door open and, leaving the keys in the lock, walked to the kitchen. As she unloaded her burden on the counter, she heard the front door bang shut.

After stashing the dairy products in the refrigerator, Huber meant to get the third grocery bag from the car when she sensed someone's presence at her back. In the split second that she turned around and saw the blow coming, she tried - - more by instinct than purpose - - to divert its force by gripping the assailant's arm.

She did not stand a chance. The cast iron frying pan came down hard on her head, mangling the skin over her forehead and one temple. It took a moment before she felt the pain, or the blood running into her eyes and covering her face. In another instant, everything was a blur. With a hushed outcry Huber slowly slid to the ground, then lay still, oblivious to the world.

Her assailant watched as a red pool formed around her head and upper body and thought, she's most likely going to bleed to death. If not, her wounds should at least keep her out of commission until after the trial. He left the heavy frying pan at her feet and on his way out, pulled the keys from the lock and placed them inside the house. Just in case someone was watching or listening, he stood at the open door, waving a good-bye toward the interior, saying, "Thanks, I'll call you next week," and quickly shut the door. Last, he pocketed the surgical gloves and walked away to his rental car parked halfway down the block.

Focused on getting out of Huber's neighborhood as fast as possible, he failed to notice that she had left her car door wide open.

CHAPTER 45

For an instant R. A. Huber was aware of pain shooting through her head as she went falling – falling – falling – then complete darkness engulfed her.

She found herself in a tunnel, devoid of light, sinking to its depth. There seemed no end to this tunnel. Occasionally, fragments of sound penetrated her world of blackness, an indication that there existed a universe outside her tunnel. There were loud sirens, oh so loud. Someone shut them off, please! Later, a momentary light flickered into her hollow, and then dark silence enclosed her again. Next time she became semi-conscious for a moment, her head felt cold and people seemed to surround her, asking questions: "Can you hear me?" "What's your name?" "Squeeze my hand." Who are these folks, she wondered. Am I in the ER? The last thing she heard was, "Skull X-ray - - type and cross match." Then she fell back into darkness. At some later time, Peter must have joined her in the abyss; she sensed his proximity.

Here we go again, Peter thought, as he kept vigil over his wife, stretched out in a hospital bed, seemingly lifeless. For the second time he went through the agony of watching over his unconscious Regula. Again, he felt powerless; she'd been placed in the hands of God and the doctors. The first incident happened nearly two years ago when a murderer she was about to expose, forced her off the road. The assailant had rammed her Buick with his mighty SUV, pushing it down a ravine, where it had overturned and landed in a ditch. She had ended up with broken bones, head wounds and a concussion. At that time, she'd been lucky that her head injuries didn't leave her brain damaged. He thought, is she going to be as fortunate now?

He stroked and squeezed her right hand for the umpteenth time, trying to get some kind of a response, but felt no stirring in the limp body. Her left hand was hooked up to an IV bottle. Seated at the edge of her bed, looking down at the partly shaved scalp and the enormous sutures across her forehead and temple, the uncanny *déjà vu* impression hit Peter anew. He bent down closer and whispered in her ear, "Love you, Regula. Now, stop the nonsense and wake up." His plea went unheard.

Peter had enjoyed a panel presentation of his fellow authors at the Writers Conference last Friday night when the authorities reached him on his cell phone with the bad news. Two-and-a-half hours later, he was at Regula's side and save for going home for showers and a few hours' sleep, he had watched over her day and night. A couple of times he thought that he'd seen her move one of her legs a tad, but he must have been mistaken.

Initially, the doctor in charge gave him a brief account of her condition. He said that Regula was lucky that she had suffered no skull fracture and her brain structure was intact. The physician assured him that so far there was no sign of active bleeding or hematoma forming. But he emphasized that the next 12 to 24 hours would be crucial in case her brain sustained contusions, which may increase pressure inside her head. Though the bleeding from external injuries seemed excessive, it was not bad enough to require a blood transfusion. When Peter asked how long it would take for her to regain consciousness, the doctor replied that it could happen at any moment, or might take days, and that she'd be in and out at first and complain of headaches. So there was nothing for Peter to do but wait.

He had called their daughter and son, as well as Andi. Even though he pointed out that Mom was unconscious and could not benefit from their visit, both insisted on coming, while Andi was devastated that she was not allowed to visit as a non-family member.

Deborah flew down from the Bay area and Ben caught a flight out of New York. They arrived at the hospital late Saturday afternoon within an hour of each other. Sunshine, as he jokingly liked to call his firstborn because of her pessimistic nature, had turned into an emotional mess and could hardly stop sobbing. She showed enough tact not to say, "I told you so," out loud, but he felt sure that was what she thought. Their daughter disapproved of her mom's private investigating business and had always maintained that it would end in disaster. Peter tried to comfort her, with little success. Ben, on the other hand, patted his dad on the shoulder and said, "Mom is tough; she'll pull through with flying colors." By Monday, Peter urged his kids to go back to their respective families, assuring them that he'd get in touch as soon as there was any change.

By Tuesday evening, Regula still was unresponsive except for an occasional moaning. Peter tried to concentrate on praying, but his mind wandered. His emotions were in constant turmoil since his life was so abruptly interrupted a few days ago. He had gone from shock to anxiety, then hope, followed by a tremendous fear of losing her, and now he was stuck at anger. Why couldn't she be content to spend her golden years like most of her contemporaries, pursuing hobbies, joining clubs, or do volunteer work? Oh no, Regula had been on a quest to become an accomplished sleuth. Never mind that she exposed herself to mortal danger on a regular basis.

His rage gave way to self-examination and he admitted that he wouldn't want her any other way. She liked her chosen occupation and was good at it. How could he even think to suggest that she should give it up? It would be comparable to her demanding that he quit writing.

The night nurse flitted in and checked Regula over. She commented, "Her neurological signs are getting better; she's definitely improving." Then she glanced his way and said, "You look exhausted, Mr. Huber. Go home and get some sleep. We know how to reach you."

CHAPTER 46

On Wednesday, August 8, Peter sat in his upright chair next to Regula's hospital bed, reading a book. After all, how long can a person stare at a non-responsive loved one? He did not know what made him look up from his read at that exact moment, but he saw her move her legs and arms; there was no mistake this time.

Then she whispered, "Peter?" And with her next breath, "Oh, my head!"

He rushed to her side and called out, "Welcome back, Regula!"

Trying to open her eyes she murmured, "Left the tunnel."

"What did you say?"

"Too bright," she stated, closed them again and fell silent.

Peter cried tears of joy. He knew from the previous experience that she would slip in and out of consciousness for a while before finally staying awake. He rang for the nurse and shared the good news.

Nurse Vicki examined her patient for pupil reaction and then calmly stated, "She's coming out of it, definitely a good sign. I'll call the physician."

Next time Regula awoke, Peter was on the phone with his daughter and spoke into it, "You can tell her directly. Here she is!" and held the phone to Regula's ear.

"Mom?"

"Yes, it's me."

"I'm so relieved to hear your voice. I love you!"

"Love you too!"

Peter reclaimed his phone and told Deborah, "Enough for now. I still need to call Ben."

It wasn't until the next day that Regula could hold a conversation for more than five minutes. Her doctor had allowed a brief interview with the police officers in charge of the assault on her. They wanted to know if she knew her attacker and she replied that she didn't remember being attacked. They apparently had checked her out and asked what kind of cases she currently worked on. She said that if her memory served her right, two jobs were under investigation at present. One was a homicide case; the other involved looking into a jewelry theft for an insurance company. When they asked for details about the murder file, she seemed to tire and her doctor came to the rescue, telling them their time was up.

Later Peter asked, "What *do* you remember of last Friday?"

"Not much. Let me think. You left for your conference in Santa Barbara, and Peggy and I played a round of golf at Snake Canyon and lunched. On the way home I made a pit stop at the office and then did some grocery shopping. That's all I remember." She paused and then asked, "Did anyone tell you what happened?"

Peter replied, "The police gave me a quick run-down when they first hit me with the horrible news. Someone whacked you over the head in our kitchen with your own cast iron frying pan. They had me check, and as far as I can tell, nothing got stolen from our home. There was no evidence of forced entry, so they assume that you let the attacker in."

"I don't recall letting anyone in."

Peter continued, "You can thank our nosy neighbor, Shannon, across the street for saving your life. She noticed that you left your car door open and thought it strange that you parked on the driveway. So she walked over to investigate. Finding a bag full of groceries on the car floor worried her and she rang the doorbell. When you didn't answer after several rings, she figured you might be ill or hurt and tried the door. It wasn't locked and she went inside. She found you lying on the kitchen floor and immediately called 911."

"Thumbs up for Shannon!"

"By the way, why *did* you park on the driveway and not pull into the garage?"

"I don't know, and yes, that is strange."

Regula closed her eyes and said, "I wish I could remember."

Peter saw that the talk had tired her and said, "Don't worry about a thing. It will all come back to you in time."

Minutes later, a hospital employee pushing a gurney showed up and then rolled her out for more test procedures. Peter suddenly realized that he was starving and headed to the cafeteria.

CHAPTER 47

During the course of the next day Regula asked, "How long have I been here?"

Peter replied, "Today is Friday. So it's been exactly a week."

"A wasted week out of a long, meaningful life hardly makes a difference," she remarked with a smirk.

He joked back, "As usual, you're ignoring *my* lost time!"

He was thrilled to see her in such good spirits. She lay propped up to an elevated position on the hospital bed but still far away from sitting up. Earlier, her attending physician's neurological examination indicated a return of normal function. He told them that he had found no evidence of any brain damage on the most recent CAT scan, but that she may still experience some headaches. Regula's condition certainly improved at a rapid speed, Peter thought, and he hummed a little tune.

His wife paid no attention to his merrymaking and mulled over the events that led to her present predicament.

She suddenly exclaimed, "Oh no! I missed my appointment with David Wachterman on Monday."

"Don't worry, Andi kept it and briefed the lawyer on what happened to you. That reminds me; Andi and I have kept in touch all week. She can't wait to see you as soon as the restriction on non-family visitors is lifted."

Regula went back to her musing and then said, "Let's assume that I let the attacker into the house - - which I am by no means ready to believe - - it makes no sense that I would have let him get into my pots and pans drawer."

"What do you mean?"

"You told me that I was hit with my cast iron frying pan. Well, I haven't used it in ages and kept it stored at the very bottom, way to the back of the drawer. He would've had to remove several other pots and pans to get at it."

"I see your point."

"You're sure he decked me with the frying pan, not some other weapon?"

"That's what the police said."

"It's almost as if he got into the house ahead of time and waited for me. That would mean he had a key." After a moment's reflection she continued, "We haven't had any workers in our home for years. Or am I wrong?"

"Can't think of any off hand."

"Besides, I know who it is, and home improvement workers making a duplicate key wouldn't apply anyway."

"You know who your attacker was?"

"I can't swear by it, but obviously my main suspect in the Rachel Penrose case tried to silence me."

"Makes sense."

Regula closed her eyes and murmured, "I can't concentrate anymore. I'm tired and my head hurts," and promptly fell asleep. Peter decided to go home and do a load of laundry.

When he returned, his spouse was wide awake and greeted him with, "I know how my suspect got into the house."

"Really?"

"I remember now why I parked on the driveway; I couldn't find the garage door opener."

"What do you mean you couldn't find it? Don't you keep it in your car?"

"Of course I do, in the glove compartment. When I got to the house on Friday, it was gone."

"So you think your attacker stole it and accessed the house through the garage?"

"Exactly. But I can't imagine how he managed it. My car hadn't been broken into, and of course the car keys were with me all day."

"You're sure you locked the car every time you left it?"

"Positive."

Peter stated, "In that case, I don't see how he could have gotten to your glove compartment."

Nurse Vicki came into the room and said, "Mr. Huber, please step out for a few minutes while I clean the patient's wounds."

As the nurse took care of the suture line, her charge suddenly burst out, "Of course, the bathroom!"

Nurse Vicki said, "Hold still, please! Do you need to use the toilet? We can't let you walk to the bathroom any time soon."

When Peter returned, Regula's head injuries were cared for and she said, "Guess what! My memory is no longer a blank from the time I reached home until hit over the head. I remember it all now. I let myself in at the front door, carrying two bags of groceries. After putting several items into the fridge, I sensed someone behind me and turned around. In the split second the assailant's arm was raised before striking me down, I saw his face!"

Not giving Peter a chance to respond, she went on, "And as far as how he got to the glove compartment of my car, it occurred to me that I left my keys in the golf bag when going to the ladies room at Snake Canyon."

He thought about this and then said, "But you had them on you; otherwise you couldn't have driven home."

"Right. It took some nerve on the suspect's part, but he had enough time to return them to the bag after getting the garage door opener, before Peggy and I came out of the bathroom."

"But Regula, in that case he must have watched you and also known your car."

"He probably followed me from our house. The invader was good; I never suspected being shadowed. And you know how I drive, always with one eye on the rear view mirror."

Peter chuckled, "To avoid getting pulled over for speeding, I'm sure!" Then he became serious and said, "Your suspect is more dangerous than I realized. I'm going to be on the alert and won't leave your side. He may try to sneak in here and finish the job."

She made light of it and said, "You've watched too many movies where the bad guys get to the patient dressed in doctor's white garb."

Regula was exhausted from so much talk and barely paid attention when Peter asked, "Why is he so determined to get rid of you? Can your testimony at Rachel's trial really destroy him?"

Hearing the word "trial", she opened her eyes wide and burst out, "Oh my God, what date do we have?"

"The 10th of August."

"The trial starts today! I need to get out of here."

"I doubt that your doctor will discharge you this soon. Don't forget what he said about going through rehab consultation first."

"Well, I just don't have time for all that."

She tried to sit up but got dizzy and dropped back onto her pillow. Frustrated, she said, "Damn it, I need to talk with Wachterman, pronto. But first, get me Andi on the phone."

CHAPTER 48

At the Pasadena Superior Court, day six of the Rachel Penrose trial resumed its process. The date was Friday, August 17, and would be the last day of Rachel's ordeal. Two witnesses were called by the defense to testify that morning, Marco Valente and Zack Jefferson. Mr. Valente's questioning concerned Cucina di Enzo, Incorporated, as well as the relationship between Steven Moretti and the board members within the company. The dispute that the Moretti brothers had in the past was also brought up. Mr. Jefferson's testimony basically consisted of his observations during the housewarming event at the Moretti residence. The roles of the lawyers were now reversed, with the defense direct examining, and the prosecution doing the cross-examining.

David Wachterman caught himself nervously checking his watch a couple of times, hoping against hope that R. A. Huber would be released from the hospital in time to testify. If not, he would have to call her assistant to the stand instead. Finally, he made the decision to first call his client, the accused. His reasoning was that the young woman's tragic demeanor might tug at the juror's heartstrings. After explaining it to Rachel, she agreed to testify.

Rachel answered the questions to his direct examination like a robot while gazing at the spectators in her arena. Earlier in the trial, the courtroom had not been full to capacity, but now nearing its end with a possible verdict in sight, there was barely an empty seat. Her parents sat in the front row. Dad gave her an encouraging nod and Mom looked as if going to burst into tears at any moment. Rachel could not bear to look at her. Tina sat next to them and avoided Rachel's eyes. Did she feel guilty about her testimony? She shouldn't; she'd said nothing but the truth. After his turn on the stand, Zack Jefferson took up a space next to his wife, Cleo, at the other side of Rachel's parents. Behind them, she spotted Jonathan, her dear faithful friend. He was the only person in the courtroom whose steady glance gave her comfort. He had been there for her in silent support all week. She was to blame for the neglect of his patients.

In the opposite camp, at the other side of the room, she saw Enzo Moretti, looking ill and frail. Poor man; she felt compassion for him. As their eyes met, his gaze was not one of accusation, only sadness. Keith sat at his side; so he came off the boat for the event, she mused. She spotted Steven's childhood friend Bart, and Cucina di Enzo's board of directors were present in full force. The rest of the observers were strangers to her, and she would not be surprised if many belonged to the media.

Wachterman had finished with Rachel and the DA cross-examined her now. At that time, Andi entered the courtroom, had a hushed conversation with the bailiff and handed him several documents and objects, then sat down in a spectator seat immediately behind Jonathan Lighthart. The bailiff gave the items to Wachterman's paralegal.

The prosecution's relentless questioning continued, "Ms. Penrose, on the day you collected your belongings from Steven Moretti's residence, you went into the backyard of the property. Correct?"

"Yes."

"What did you do there?"

"I dug up my herb garden."

"Did you go near the oleander plant?"

"No."

The cross-examination went on and on. When preparing her for the trial, her attorney had coached her to give only "yes" or "no" answers whenever possible, should she be called to testify. That suited her fine. She was so tired of it all. Would the trial ever end? It had only been a week since the start of it, but felt like years. She sought Jonathan's eyes and his reassuring glance gave her comfort and strength.

The judge said, "Answer the question, Ms. Penrose."

Rachel tried to focus on the prosecutor and said, "Sorry, what was the question?"

"Were you extremely angry with your fiancé when you found him with Ms. Dewitt?"

"Yes."

"To the point of wanting him dead?"

"Yes."

"Did you kill your fiancé?"

She shook her head.

"I repeat. Did you kill Steven Moretti?"

"No."

The DA grilled Rachel further, rendering her near exhaustion by the time he was done with her. The judge had to tell her twice that she could step down before it registered, and she made a shaky retreat.

At the defense table, the paralegal leaned toward her boss, David Wachterman, in a huddle, who then promptly asked the judge for a sidebar.

When the lengthy whispering between the two lawyers and the judge stopped, his Honor looked up at the clock and said, "Let's recess for lunch." And addressing the prosecution and defense attorneys, he stated, "I'll see you gentlemen in my chamber."

Twenty minutes later, the judge and the lawyers had finished watching a video in the former's chamber which David Wachterman had asked to be admitted into evidence, and he submitted four documents as exhibits.

The DA spoke first and said, "I protest the video's submission! Coming forth with something this unorthodox at the last minute is contrary to procedure."

Wachterman countered, "The witness was scheduled to testify. She can't help having been brutally assaulted and is now being detained in the hospital to recuperate from severe injuries."

The judge held up his hand and said, "Gentlemen, please! We all want to arrive at the truth. Under the circumstances, I'll allow the video and the documents to be entered as evidence."

The prosecutor thought, it is clear that the judge already made up his mind what the truth is. He knew better than to voice his opinion, though, and hoped that the jury would see it differently.

CHAPTER 49

Everyone filed back into the courtroom, and when the judge made his entrance the court convened.

David Wachterman handed the judge some papers and said, "I submit four documents into evidence, which your Honor has approved and the prosecution has accepted: Exhibit A is a handwritten affidavit; Exhibit B, a letter from Tea Brewer in England; Exhibit C is a copy of an e-mail; and Exhibit D, a letter from a physician at Merida Hospital."

His Honor browsed through the documents and then said, "Proceed."

Wachterman faced the jury and announced, "I'll go into specifics about said documents later, but first will present you with a video. It is the testimony in an affidavit from a witness who was scheduled to appear before you today but cannot be present. The affidavit is handwritten, made under oath in the presence of two witnesses, and notarized." With a few commands on his laptop he activated the video, and a scene on the big screen, which had been set up during the lunch recess, came into focus.

The camera first scanned a hospital room with three people standing next to the patient's bed and then zoomed in on the woman propped up in her hospital bed. Transparent adhesive tape across her forehead and one temple held together the extensive stitches.

The woman in the video was sworn in by the notary public and then read from her handwritten affidavit, "My name is R. A. Huber and I am a private investigator. Below is a list of my statements of facts: Number 1: I was hired to find Steven Moretti's killer. Number 2: Oleander grows on the median strip in the small town of Kurtsbad, along Pacific Highway in San Diego County. Number 3: Tea Brewer of England shipped loose leaf tea to Keith Moretti in Fort Lauderdale, Florida, on March 14; its estimated arrival in the US was March 21 – 24. Number 4: Steven Moretti received a tea shipment on March 29. Number 5: On July 5, I sent an e-mail to all suspects, aimed in particular at my main suspect. Number 6: On August 3, my main suspect attacked me at my residence."

Huber looked briefly into the camera and then continued reading, "Now that I stated the facts, I'd like to give my opinion as to their merit. I am convinced that Keith Moretti poisoned his brother. It is my conviction that he got the idea when Rachel Penrose jokingly mentioned that she would add oleander to her fiancé's tea if he did not behave. I believe that Keith Moretti helped himself to the poisonous substance from one of the oleander bushes in Kurtsbad. On March 23 or 24, he picked up the tea package sent to his PO Box in Florida, added the poisonous oleander, and mailed it to his brother, before boarding his ship headed for the Caribbean. My e-mail message was meant as bait. Keith Moretti took it and launched his assault, trying to prevent me from testifying at Rachel Penrose's trial.

"The material provided for in this affidavit is true to the best of my knowledge. 11:00 a.m. on Wednesday, August 15, 2012 at Merida Hospital."

She signed the document in plain view of the camera: Regula Agatha Huber.   And so did the witnesses, Antoinette LeJeune and Nurse Vicki Johnson. The notary public put his official stamp at the bottom of the affidavit and then also dated and signed it.

The screen went blank and for a moment total silence engulfed the courtroom. The full meaning of what they had just seen and heard dawned on the jury and the rest of the assembly. Even before Huber mentioned Keith's name in the affidavit, he made a quick exit, but got no farther than the hallway where the bailiff apprehended him.

In the courtroom, David Wachterman showed each exhibit on the screen where everyone could read the documents for themselves.   Exhibit D, the letter from Huber's hospital doctor, simply stated that she was of sound mind.

He gave the jury time to read and ponder each document on the big screen and then said, "The defense rests."

Now that both sides had presented their evidence and came to rest, the attorneys proceeded to their closing arguments. The defense went first.

David Wachterman addressed the jury. "The affidavit video you saw a moment ago speaks for itself. You will be given the written document plus the other exhibit documents for your inspection when you are sent to deliberate. The evidence against Rachel Penrose that the prosecution presented to you in the course of this trial is all circumstantial. There are no eye witnesses who saw her poison Steven Moretti's tea. She lived in his house; it is only natural that her DNA was found on his property, but none of it can be linked to his tea or the tea canister. The prosecution may argue that the evidence brought forward by R. A. Huber against Keith Moretti is also circumstantial.

But, never forget, the attack on Huber by Keith Moretti was a direct act to silence her."

He looked at each juror in turn and then continued, "In order to find Rachel Penrose guilty of the crime, she must be proven guilty *beyond a reasonable doubt*. The prosecution has fallen short of that burden of proof. Therefore, you must acquit the defendant and find her *not guilty*."

The district attorney had the last word with his own closing argument. He strutted in front of the jury box and said, "Mr. Wachterman is correct; all the evidence his witness, R. A. Huber, referred to in her affidavit is circumstantial. Unfortunately, I am unable to cross-examine the lady. Given the chance, I'd question her about Exhibit C, her e-mail sent to Keith Moretti. To refresh your memories, I will read the e-mail message to you. I quote: 'I have a good lead concerning a possible solution to Steven Moretti's homicide. This murder plot goes deeper than at first glance. I've uncovered a dark secret. And here is another hint: There are many places besides Steven's backyard where oleander bushes are grown. I happen to believe that I know where the killer found the oleander leaves that were added to the victim's tea.'

"Now, ladies and gentlemen of the jury, these are empty allegations, pure and simple. What dark secret? And what about these alleged oleander bushes? Even if the oleander in the victim's tea came from one of the plants grown in the town of Kurtsbad, the private investigator had no proof that it was Keith Moretti who seized it. Another fact comes to mind: How can we be sure that R. A. Huber recognized her assailant?"

He continued, "As far as we know, Keith Moretti had no motive to kill his brother. We learned from the testimony of Marco Valente that he had no claim to Cucina di Enzo, Incorporated, and did not stand to benefit financially from

Steven Moretti's death. But Rachel Penrose had a strong motive to murder her fiancé, and we heard from the key witness, Jasmine Dewitt, that she threatened to kill him. In the name of justice you must find the defendant, Rachel Penrose *guilty*."

The judge then gave closing instructions to the jury, reminding them that they must reach a unanimous verdict, and sent them to the deliberation room.

It took the jury only two hours to return with a "not guilty" verdict.

EPILOGUE

Six months later on Valentine's Day of the next year, R. A. Huber sat in her office and labored over the tedious chore of sorting through her records. In spite of having an accountant doing her taxes, she was still left with the job of gathering information and adding up the figures around this time every year.

She had long recovered from her head injuries and thankfully did not suffer any lasting effect from the attack. Her previously shoulder length hair that used to frame her face had now been cut into a short do, with bangs covering the scars on her forehead.

A couple of unexpected visitors appeared at the door, and Jonathan Lighthart said, "I hope we're not intruding. Rachel and I were in the neighborhood and decided to say hello."

"Not at all, I'm delighted to see you both. Come on in and have a seat," Huber replied and shoved forms, bank records, and receipts aside. She offered them coffee or tea, but they declined, having come straight from lunch.

Huber looked Rachel over. This young woman was a different person from the passive and lifeless creature she remembered interviewing last spring. The Rachel facing her now looked confident, well-balanced, and happy.

She said, "You look radiant!"

Then she glanced at the doctor who seemed in a chipper mood of his own. She grinned and said, "Are congratulations in order?"

"You bet," he replied. Appropriate for Valentine's Day, I popped the question over lunch and Rachel accepted."

Rachel said, "Jonathan has been my best friend all my life, but until recently, I was too stupid to see that he is also the man for me."

Then she said, "We basically stopped by to thank you again. If not for you, I'd be locked up in prison, or worse. And I'm real sorry that you were attacked by Keith, landing you in the hospital."

"The risk of getting into harm's way is part of my job, so don't worry about that."

Jonathan inquired, "In the video we saw that you had sustained head injuries, but you didn't go into details about the attack. What weapon did he use?"

Huber chuckled and said, "He hit me over the head with a cast iron frying pan. Fitting for a cook, don't you think?"

Then she became somber and addressed Rachel, "I'd like to bring something up, just to satisfy my curiosity. You must have known that you acted guilty when I interviewed you, and that your guilty attitude also showed when you talked with your attorney or anyone else. Why didn't you proclaim your innocence and simply state that you *did not* kill Steven Moretti?"

"But that's just it; I *did* feel guilty," Rachel replied. "I wished him dead with all my heart. When I was in the yard that day, digging up my herb garden, I went over to the oleander bush and fantasized about snipping off some leaves to add to Steven's tea to poison him in that way. Then, when he died, I felt happy about it. And since nobody else seemed to have a motive, I started to wonder if I had actually done it and then blocked it from memory. So you see, I felt guilty and needed to be punished."

Jonathan said, "I've been telling Rachel more than once that there is a huge difference between wishing someone dead and actually killing the person. I think in the last few months I've finally convinced her of her innocence."

Then he said, "Since financial gain is ruled out, what motive did Keith have?"

"Jealousy. He was extremely envious of his brother."

"How did you figure that out?"

"When Andi and I talked to him on board ship and I inquired into his childhood, it became clear that he felt inferior to his brother and resented him. But it was not until much later, when I sat at my desk one day and reflected on the interview, that his words 'jealousy is a sickness' took on a whole new meaning. Keith, of course, referred to Rachel as being jealous, but the truth suddenly hit me at that moment."

Jonathan said, "I was on pins and needles up until the very end of the trial. It could have easily gone the other way had it not been for your affidavit. And the prosecutor made a valid point in his closing argument; your e-mail wasn't clear. Explain a couple of things, please. First, how did you come to the conclusion that the oleander leaves came from a bush in Kurtsbad?"

Huber explained, "I could have never proved it, but here is how I put the puzzle together. Enzo Moretti talked about a car chase in progress shutting the 5 Freeway down when he and Keith were driving home to San Diego after the housewarming. They had to take surface streets with traffic being slow and congested, especially going through Kurtsbad. I drove that same stretch after my interview with the senior Moretti, but I only remembered much later that I saw a row of oleander plants growing on the median strip in that small town.

"Once I suspected Keith of the crime, I tried to put myself in his shoes, and here is what I ended up with. Keith had just heard Rachel make a joking remark about adding poisonous oleander to Steven's tea that day. And of course, he also saw the oleander bush in their yard and knew what the plant looked like. I believe that making peace with his brother a few months before was only a pretense in order to get back in touch with him. Murder was on his mind, but he had as yet to come up with a foolproof plan. Imagine how thrilled he must have been when, slowly driving by that median strip, he suddenly figured out a way to commit the crime, alibi and all."

"I'm still not sure how he did it."

"Here is how I pictured it. Keith went back to the place later, probably during the night when people of the small bedroom community were asleep, and snipped off a small amount of oleander leaves. Next, he waited until the timing was right and then ordered the loose leaf tea that Steven usually drank from Tea Brewer."

Jonathan asked, "What do you mean with 'timing was right'?"

Huber went to her file cabinet, took out the Rachel Penrose file, saying, "I need to refresh my memory pertaining to dates." When she found the corresponding documents, she explained, "Let me backtrack a little. When I talked to Keith on board ship during the Alaskan cruise, he said he had been on a two-week New Zealand/ Australia cruise route ending in Sidney on April 9, which put him in those waters from March 26 – April 9. His father told me that right before the Australian run, Keith had been on a few Western Caribbean round trips out of Fort Lauderdale, Florida.

"In their letter to me, Tea Brewer stated that they shipped the loose leaf tea to Keith, addressing it to a PO Box in Fort Lauderdale. I did some research, and Keith's cruise ship returned from its round trip back to Fort Lauderdale on March 23. So here is what he did: On March 23 or 24, he picked up the tea package at his PO Box, mixed in the poisonous oleander leaves, and then sent the package to his brother. By the time the deadly shipment was flown to California, Keith cooked his first formal dinner on international waters on his way to New Zealand."

"Yes, I get it now." And after a moment's reflection he asked, "How did you manage to get the shipping data from Tea Brewer? Had they no qualms about giving out client information?"

"That was easy," Huber replied, "I stated in my letter that I acted on behalf of Keith Moretti, who was at sea at the moment. I wrote that Keith needed the dates of each tea shipment made by them for his records. In their response letter they stressed that they had only received one order and made one sole shipment. Tea Brewer processed the parcel by air from England to his PO Box in Fort Lauderdale on March 14."

Huber closed the file and continued, "When I learned from Mr. Moretti, Sr., that Marco Valente visited him in San Diego on a regular basis, I briefly transferred my suspicion to him, thinking that the new CEO tried to influence the old gentleman to bequeath him the company. That idea only lasted a moment; there were too many facts that pointed to Keith as the killer."

Rachel said, "Enzo Moretti passed away in October. I wish he could have been spared the news that his younger son was his brother's murderer." And shedding a tear she added, "The dear man called me soon after the trial and apologized for having thought I killed Steven."

Jonathan squeezed her hand and then went on, "The other thing I'm curious about: What *was* that dark secret you uncovered?"

Huber said, "That is also something I will never be able to prove since it is basically just my gut feeling. I suspect that Keith also killed his sister."

Rachel and Jonathan both gasped in horror.

Huber went on, "I believe that instead of coming to the rescue of his sister as he claimed, he actually held her down under water until she drowned. I learned that he and Jennifer quarreled and she threatened to tell on Keith about his experimenting with drugs. When interviewing Keith, it was obvious to me that he had always envied his siblings. His jealousy as a youngster ran deep, and I suspect his resentment grew even more profound as he matured. I also have an inkling that Steven guessed the truth about Jennifer's drowning, but of course that is pure speculation. Anyway, it happened over 17 years ago and even though there is no statute of limitations for murder, the case is cold and would be impossible to prove."

All three fell silent, each preoccupied with their own train of thought.

Then Rachel asked, "What is Keith's fate now?"

"He has been charged and arrested. There was an arraignment, and I understand that he pleaded guilty in the hope of a lighter sentence. I am unfamiliar with the outcome of his plea-bargaining, though."

Huber absent-mindedly picked up the black rook off her chessboard and twirling the piece around in her fingers remarked, "In my opinion, Keith's hatred of Steven intensified over the years and became an obsession in the end. It is the age-old story of Cain and Abel."

Jonathan stated, "Yes, but with a slight difference; in our case *both* brothers were flawed."

If you enjoyed reading this book, please give it a review on www.amazon.com.

R. A. Huber Mysteries by Alice Zogg

Guilty or Not
Murder at the Cubbyhole
Revamp Camp
Final Stop Albuquerque
The Fall of Optimum House
The Lonesome Autocrat
Tracking Backward
Turn the Joker Around
Reaching Checkmate

Available at www.amazon.com,
www.barnesandnoble.com
and other vendors.